THE YELLOW JOCK CHRONICLES

Volume One: Jockstrap Epiphany

A Journey into Self-Awareness, Discovery and Acceptance:
An Obsession with Jockstraps and Piss-Lust

First Edition

Published by The Nazca Plains Corporation
Las Vegas, Nevada
2007

ISBN: 978-1-934625-28-6

Published by
The Nazca Plains Corporation ®
4640 Paradise Rd, Suite 141
Las Vegas NV 89109-8000

PUBLISHER'S NOTE
The Yellow Jock Chronicles – Volume One is a work of fiction created wholly by *Matthew M. Schiffmann's* imagination. All characters are fictional and any resemblance to any persons living or deceased is purely by accident. No portion of this book reflects any real person or events.

Cover, Fleshblack Images
Art Director, Blake Stephens

DEDICATION

For "Dean"
Requiescat in Pacem
Et Lux Perpetua Luceat Eis.

THE YELLOW JOCK CHRONICLES

Volume One: Jockstrap Epiphany

A Journey into Self-Awareness, Discovery and Acceptance:
An Obsession with Jockstraps and Piss-Lust

First Edition

Matthew M. Schiffmann

CONTENTS

SOMETHING NEW

I first met Dean Cordell in Chicago. My supposed 'best friend' had convinced me to take a weekend trip, skipping away from our local haunts in suburban Minneapolis with almost no preparation. Oh we'd done such things before, including Chicago, but this was different. We had a suite lined up, paid for a full week stint.

But that was all. No food, no smokes, no liquor. At eighteen I was already becoming a pretty heavy-duty boozer, and so was Tim. He was about 6 months older than me, and we were of legal age, but in those days it didn't matter much anyhow. I looked mature, and had almost never been asked for ID for anything. This time wouldn't be any different. Besides, the pub we usually partied at was right in the hotel building, just around the corner, and the staff, patrons and locals all knew us both.

It didn't take me too long to agree to going; I packed up a small grip and headed to the airport. I'd called ahead and made a fictitious reservation on a commuter airline, and the stand-by ticket to Chicago was less than $30. Two hours later I was deposited at Meigs Field, and walked the 10 or so blocks to the Maryland Hotel. Tim was already there, having taken an earlier hop into town, and had paid the rent for the suite. He grinned as I came into the room.

"GIRLFRIEND!" he crooned. He could be such a fuckin' queen. 'Tim LaRoque;' it suited him. It pissed me off when he went into the feminine mode, but that was just him. We'd been buddies since 8th grade. We'd been each other's 'first;' when my folks left me home alone for my 18th birthday weekend, we'd finally had the opportunity to learn to fuck like men.

"You made it! I wasn't sure you'd come after all that _drama_ with Mike and all." Tim was referring to an incident of 4 weeks earlier, when I got into some heavy shit with a golden-gloves wanna-be I'd met in the lounge of the Maryland. The guy had been hotter than hell, awesome body and cock for days, but a total psycho. He liked to bottom and that was fine with me, but he liked some really rough action. I wasn't up for his kind of play, and it had gotten to where he wanted to beat the shit out of me just to prove how wild he could be, because I didn't want to beat the shit out of him. Rough and tumble, including fisticuffs, was his idea of 'foreplay.' Somehow I'd gotten out of there intact, and I wasn't going anywhere near that asshole again.

"Hell with that noise. Mike can go back to Berwyn and fuck himself with a wine bottle for all I care." I did still have his number in my trick-book though... just in case.

"I'm going to get myself set here _girl_ and go down to Alfie's for the lunch crowd. I can still meet up with Jerry before 4:00." Tim was already decked up, and there was no way he was going to wait for me. "Jerry's got a real big hot one you know. Damn it's nice. Big nose, big hands, big ditter..." I gave him a sideways glance and slight smirk.

"Oh I know," he said. "Size queen. So what? Here in the Windy Mindy City, EVERYONE is a queen. Size queen, drag queen, street queen, shower queen... who cares? It's whatever you're into."

"Yeah right," I said. Jerry was a hot one, that was true. Body, boner, brains, brawn and big bucks too. Tim could pick them, there was no doubt about that. "Then I'll catch up with you guys down there."

He nodded, fluffed his hair once more and swished out the door. I took a few minutes getting acquainted with the seedy rooms and putting my gear away in my room. The Maryland was a flophouse, both hotel, motel, bar, restaurant and weekly apartments too. It was right up our alley at the moment.

I chose an outfit a bit different than my usual. Nice business slacks, a pressed shirt, but I skipped the tie. I wanted to look like something more than a bar hustler, regardless of what anyone thought. I wouldn't have admitted to hustling anyhow, and Tim had endless euphemisms for his actions. Last time we'd been to Alfie's, another customer asked me about him.

"He's working with the Lila Marks agency; he's a model," I'd said.

"Hmmm... or _purports_ to be," the hunky guy had responded. I almost laughed, but I didn't want to make it too clear that I was in fact 'with' Tim in the endeavor. The same afternoon I'd met up with a man who'd attended a class in German Lit with me at the University. Small world; I'd wanted to get some dick from him back then, and this time I finally did. Nice big cock, lots of precum and a hot hairy butt that welcomed my invasion with utmost pleasure. I should've kept after him... ah me, the ones that get away.

I adjusted my attire, the bulge of my jock filled with my basket cinched in a leather cock strap pushing out in the fine wool of my slacks. The crisp white shirt showed my slightly hairy chest to full advantage, and I straightened up. Not bad; I was over 6 feet tall, about 185 pounds and nicely shaped. I locked the door as I left and headed to the elevator. Four minutes later I was entering Alfie's.

The doorman stopped me for a moment. "Sir... SIR! You do realize this is a GAY BAR?"

"Um, uh... yeah...?"

"Oh yeah, I remember you. You've been here before..." I nodded and continued in. Not a bad idea, I thought, warn the businessmen BEFORE someone gets hit on who doesn't wanna be hit on. Just avoid the fist-fight before it happens. Smart door guy.

Tim was in a corner booth with Jerry. The lecherous lawyer had an arm around him, and was stroking the inside of his thigh. Ho hum, already. "Hey there," I said.

"Oh hey Matt. You know Jerry?" We shook hands, yes, we'd already met. I wouldn't've minded a romp with Jerry at all, but he wasn't interested in me. Too much a <u>total</u> top I guess; not that I would have said 'no' to taking his fat cock up my ass.

'*Friends with benefits*,' Tim called it. Yeah sure. But I was sure Tim had told him about our interactions... Tim loved me to fuck him, or had at least enjoyed it when he couldn't get anyone else.

I sat and had a drink with them. Jerry had an open bar tab going and he wouldn't care how much I knocked onto it. Free drinks until they left, so that was OK. After the courtesy talk I excused myself and went to the leaning rail, the 'corral' beside the dance floor. I took a typical pose, ready, willing, able and oh-so-available. I checked out the men poised around the lounge, those dancing, those necking, and those looking for company just like me.

My gaze focused at last on a good-looking man of about 30 or so. Maybe a bit more, but I liked them mature. Body hair and experience, just what I wanted. He made eye contact and then smiled. I nodded, and quickly he came over to talk to me. In the unspoken etiquette of the gay bar, I knew that meant he'd be fucking me, not the other way around. Fine as well, tonight I was more than ready to bottom. I hoped he was well hung, that he'd go a long time. I was my turn to have my asshole stretched open.

"Hey there!" He stuck out a hand, and introduced himself. "Dean; how you doing?" I shook hands firmly, letting him stroke my hand and forearm as we broke off.

"Nice to meet you Dean! I'm Matt." I smiled, he was just what I wanted to play with. He was hot.

He smiled back, then leaned against the rail alongside me. "So what's up tonight? It's still early, but this scene is tired isn't it?"

"You said it man! No shit." I took a drag from my cigarette, then looked at him again. "It gets old real fast huh?"

"Sure does."

"I just got into town though, kinda stuck right here though. I'm staying here at the Maryland."

His eyes lit up above his moustache. "Cool! I'm in town for a bit also, but I didn't get a room. I live out by Rockford." He leaned back a bit, showing the nice full bulge in the front of his Levi's. Nice bulge. Oh there was plenty of man-meat in there. Plenty. And he didn't waste any time.

"So... you want to have a couple more drinks here, or maybe go upstairs to your place?"

That was interesting, the guy inviting me up to my own room. But I also knew that meant he was that much more the dominant man. Woof! That was hot too... he was going to take me to my own place and take over. I was ready.

"Um, let's get a few beers to go, then go up, how about that?"

"Great!" he replied, "A few beers to have up there, take our time. Perfect!" He motioned to a bar waiter and ordered a 6-pack to go. "We've got this one, maybe one more here?" I nodded and the waiter brought us each another long-neck. We made small talk as we drank those, then went to the bar to pick up our travelers. I put them on Jerry's tab and tipped out; we headed for the door.

"Just a second," I said, remembering Tim and Jerry. "I gotta make sure we have plenty of privacy, you know?"

Dean nodded, and I went back to the corner booth. Oh indeed, we'd have privacy, they were also getting ready to leave, heading uptown to a show.

"See you tomorrow sometime _girl_!" Tim sang, and I spun on my heel to catch up to Dean. He was waiting at the door, the bulge in his jeans that much thicker I could see. Indeed, _he_ was ready. Damn, this was going to be a good one! I felt a twitch in my cock and asshole at the same time; I was ready for action too.

We walked out into the late twilight and up the half-block into the hotel lobby. The desk clerk gave us nary a look as we got into the elevator and headed up to the 18th floor. Dean pawed at me in the car, grabbing a handful of my ass through the fabric of my slacks. It felt nice, it was like he cupped my hole... my asshole was nestled into the palm of his hand. I liked it; I groped him back, and the fullness of that bulge was then apparent to me. Big, _very_ big; this would surely test my endurance and abilities.

I'd had some big cocks up my ass, but I could tell this was easily going to be the biggest so far. I wanted to see it, taste it, hold it... take it inside me. I nestled up to him, and he spun me around and caught me in a tight hot kiss. His tongue burrowed into my mouth, all the way to the back of my throat. I sucked and smooched, pressing my body against his. The strength of his muscles was intoxicating, his scent... he was fine. I leaned back, then stroked the front of his jeans again. He reached over and tugged the STOP button on the control panel. The elevator jolted and stopped. I was a bit hesitant, but he kissed me again. Then he pressed on my shoulders, lightly. Very lightly, but his message was clear, and I dropped to my knees.

I ran my hands up the front of the tight denim, then began to tug at the buttons. Five-oh-ones, wow. I'd only seen them once before. That too was hot. I got the fly open and Dean unbuckled his belt. I tugged lightly at the waistband and down they came. There it was.

Oh god what a sight! His magnificent cock flopped out in front of me, easily 9 full inches. Thick, veiny and already just about totally hard, it smelled like man-fur. His thick bush reeked with clean manscent. I was in heaven. I opened my mouth and took in the head. I licked the slit, tasting a nice drop of manly precum. I opened wider and he slid in... more and more. He filled my mouth and yet almost half his cock was still out in the open. It was delicious.

He took hold of my head with his hands and forced more of his manhood into my mouth. I took it, began to gag, but forced myself to take more. To suck, to allow him to face fuck me there in the elevator. I gulped and gagged, and took more, and more. He bucked and jammed himself almost to the root, the head of his fat dick slipping between my tonsils and down my throat.

"Ah yeah buddy! That's it! Eat that cock man! Eat it!"

I gulped and sucked and took more. I wanted to get up to my room, but I wasn't ready to stop this scene. It was fine, hot and horny. I loved sucking Dean. I wanted it to go on as long as he wanted... when he wanted more, he'd let me know.

And it wasn't much longer. He pulled himself out of my mouth with a plop, and held my head in his paws. He tugged me back to my feet and I stood up. With a flick Dean pushed the STOP button back in and the car again moved upwards. Another 30 seconds and we stopped, the doors opening on the 18th floor. We held hands as we walked down the hallway towards my room. The beer bottles clinked in the bag as I unlocked the room. Dean stood beside me as I opened the door, his fat cock still sticking out the opening of his jeans. Ready. Oozing. Beautiful.

We entered and once more Dean spun me into a tight manly embrace, kissing me hard and deep. I whipped the door closed and instantly was on my knees sucking and slurping his hot organ. He was writhing and bucking himself out of his clothes, then began pulling at mine. Within a minute or so we were naked, his furry chest heaving in front of me. He pulled me up to my feet, then moved me toward the bed.

I sat at the edge, and once more took his fat cock into my mouth. His hands were all over me, down my back, across my chest, gripping my own not-inconsiderable cock. He gripped my thigh, then swung my legs up. There was a slight clatter as he found the lube and poppers on the table beside the bed. He handed me the little brown bottle as he slapped some of the slick grease onto his cock. I twisted the cap and took a deep huff, first on the right, then the left. I felt the rush take over as Dean slathered a nice gob of lube on my asshole. He lifted my legs onto his shoulders and I felt his cockhead against my pucker. Then...

White lightening.

He thrust his hips forward and slammed that huge cock up my ass in one total, mind-wrenching stroke. I yelped, then screamed aloud.

"OH MY GOD! OH GOD DEAN! AHHHHHHHHHH!"

He pulled back and then did it again. The pain, the sensations were overwhelming. I'd been fucked, but oh shit! I was being _fucked_ and there was nothing I was going to do about any of it! And I'd gone along with it, _encouraged_ him; there was going to be no stopping Dean at this point. I knew that much. I gritted my teeth and whined, bucked my hips upward in uncontrolled reaction, and he jammed into me a third time.

"OH GOD MAN YOU'RE SPLITTING ME OPEN! OH GOD DEAN, STOP! PLEASE!"

He paused, then ground his cock slowly in me up to the limit. It was hot, excruciating, wild. He leaned over me closely, his face right up to mine, breathing into my mouth. He kissed me again, quickly, then looked into my eyes as I tried to writhe away. "Here," he said. "It doesn't hurt."

"Oh god Dean, please! Please!"

"LOOK INTO MY EYES," he said clearly, powerfully. "Look..."

I looked into his clear blue eyes, sparkling in the dim light.

"Say it with me... It does NOT hurt. Say it."

I nodded, then spoke with him. "It does not hurt..."

"Yeah that's it. Again. Say it _with_ me, and _mean_ it." We spoke together.

"It doesn't hurt. IT DOES NOT HURT." And suddenly, it was true! My asshole relaxed, opened, welcomed him. I opened to him and he drew back, almost to the point of popping out of me. Then he thrust in again, hard. He thrust into me with all his might and oh GOD! It was heaven. It didn't hurt a bit, it was something beyond 'pain.' I groaned in ecstasy.

"Yeah that's it!" he encouraged. "That's it boy, open that hole!" and he stroked, rammed, plowed into me. "Open your asshole boy, that's it. OPEN UP for me!" He fucked me with strength and power. He went deep, he fucked hard, he reamed me. He opened my asshole wider and deeper than it had ever been. I bucked my hips up in rhythm to his thrusts, taking him, helping him to fuck me.

"Oh god Dean! Oh god man, FUCK ME!" I bucked, and writhed, my hands gripped his ass cheeks as I pulled him harder into my body. He jammed himself in to the hilt, then swung me over, heaving himself onto the bed at last, yet without letting his dick slide out of my hole. Quickly he positioned me on the bed, himself atop me solidly, then resumed his attack on my asshole.

"Yeah Matt, that's it boy! Take it! You can take it, you love it don't you?

Tell me you love it, tell me you WANT it!"

"Oh yeah man! Fuck yeah Dean, I love it! I love your COCK man, fuck me! I love the way you're FUCKING me man! Fuck me hard, harder man! *FUCK ME!*."

He smiled and did what I told him. He fucked me hard, and then slammed himself in me harder. The sensations, the overwhelming totality of his rapine fucking was wonderful. His cock was a weapon: it was a tool, a battering ram, a pole, a reamer. I was oozing and rock hard myself, my cock rubbing against the fur on his belly as he stroked and thrust into my ass over and over. I wanted it all. All.

And he gave it. He thrust into me and a low moan began in his throat, a growl as he neared completion. His cock swelled inside me and I thought 'This is IT. He really IS going to split the sides of my rectum...' He thrust again and the beads of sweat on his forehead sparkled. He ground in to the limit and howled.

"OH GOD YEAH MATT! Take it buddy! TAKE IT! I'm gonna cum, I'm gonna Cum! Oh yeah I'm cumming boy, yeah I'M CUMMING! HERE IT IS!"

I bucked and pressed up against him as hard as I could, my fingers sunk into the flesh of his ass, holding him TIGHT, hard inside me. He came. He spurted and came, and his body thrashed and writhed in whelming pleasure as he poured his juice deep up inside my guts. He came. And came. And came more. He pumped gob after hot gob of his spooge inside me and I loved it. I wanted it, and he poured himself into me.

As if in slow motion it went on and on, then wound down. Slowly, we eased into a heap of sweaty flesh, his cock still deep within me, his cum leaking around the base of his dick from my well-worked hole. He collapsed atop me, my arms holding him close. We kissed.

Finally, slowly, he pulled back. Back and out. I felt empty, incomplete.

I had always known fucking, _being_ fucked, could be that fine, that awesome, but hadn't lived it. And I wasn't inexperienced... but everything up till this moment had been only practice, rehearsal. And now, _Dean_. I wanted more.

He laid me back on the bed and fingered my asshole, pulling out a gob of his own cum. He laid it across the thick fur of his moustache and leaned in; I kissed him again and savored it. His cum from my asshole. Obscene, beautiful, powerful. Hell yeah! He did it again. I loved it.

He stroked my body, and took my cock into his hot, strong hand. He jacked me slowly, slipping up and down the shaft in my precum. I oozed more, leaking steadily. I moaned, then pushed my hips upward. He stopped.

"No, I don't want you to cum yet," He said. "I can go a lot longer, if you can..." I smiled.

"Sure! I'll wait! Let's enjoy it. I'd like to suck you again, but..." I trailed off. He took the hint.

"Yeah I'd like that. Let's go hop in the shower, get me cleaned up so you can have some more dick. You like it, don't you? You want more of my cock, don't you?"

"Yes, I do," I said softly.

"Then tell me. Ask me for more..."

"Dean... Dean, can I have more of it? Can I suck you again?"

"Of what?"

"Your cock man, your COCK. Let me suck it more, OK? Please? Then maybe, _Fuck_ me again? Please?"

"Sure thing Matt, you can have more. I'm going to give you everything I got. Everything. Come on."

He rose and pulled me up to my feet. The sudden stab of pain through my belly let me know I'd been fucked soundly, but it wasn't unpleasant. Intense, powerful, yes; bad, no. It was pain, but a kind I'd not experienced before. I liked it. Every step reminded me of Dean's cock slamming into my guts.

We went into the bathroom and turned on the water. Steam filled the room. The frosted glass above the mirror filtered the light, only one of the 4 bulbs was working and the room was bathed in a soft glow. It was romantic, sensual... horny and suggestive, like the shower room in school. I had a momentary memory of Bob Smith, a beautiful football player in high school. I'd had PE with him, and often sneaked admiring glances at his body in the showers. He knew it too, and enjoyed showing off.

Dean pulled the curtain back and stepped into the shower. I followed. We kissed and held one another, quickly rinsing off. He held me, and once more the slight pressure on my shoulders told me to go down on him. I complied. Once more his cock was rock hard, standing straight out nine full inches. The water ran down his chest, around his bush as I took him into my mouth and suckled.

He began stroking in and out of my mouth, face fucking me slowly. He took his time and enjoyed every millimeter of his own dick exploring the recesses of my mouth. He thrust into the back of my throat, then to the side, then slid across my tongue. I sucked and held him, I put my hands up against his furry belly, like a supplicant, reaching up. I worshipped; in that moment I loved him so.

"Yeah that's it boy," he said. "Go for it, take it. Suck me boy, that's right. Take it all now, ALL THE WAY down," as he held the back of my head and SHOVED himself totally down my throat. I swallowed, gulped and took him. He face fucked me, using me. It was great.

Slowly he pulled back letting his cock flop out and hang before me. His eyes twinkled, then narrowed slightly. I didn't know what he was thinking, I only hoped I was sucking and offering myself well enough to give him half the pleasure and joy he was giving me. He reached forward and offered me the brown bottle.

"Here, take a big hit," he commanded. I did; taking double and triple snorts on each nostril, then he took it back from me and huffed twice himself. His cock jumped and then...

A spurt of golden piss shot out of his dickhead and splashed onto my chest. I gasped in shock.

"Hey stay still!" he barked, and I instantly did. I was scared, amazed, horrified. He let his cock point outward again, then it again began to flow. "Look at it," he said. I watched.

He pointed it at me and hosed my chest, my bush, my own cock. He timed his spurts wonderfully; hot spurt, then pause. Spurt, pause. Suddenly I was totally rock hard. It worried me, why was this flow of PISS so hot? Why was I reacting so intensely to it? I'd seen guys piss many times, of course. Yeah it was nice, I liked to watch, but damn! He lifted his cock and splashed his stream up, across my neck, onto my face.

"That's it, now... OPEN YOUR MOUTH," he ordered.

I was aghast, but it was as if an unseen, unstoppable force compelled me.

I leaned back slightly, let my eyes droop half closed and _opened my mouth_.

His aim was perfect, and he shot a stream of hot golden piss right into my mouth. Across my tongue.

I was so shocked, I was only barely aware of the taste. But it was not bad at all, it wasn't horrible or strange in the least. Suddenly, it was nice. Salty. Golden and rich. It tasted like *Dean*, like Dean's cock, like the scent of hundreds of men's rooms I'd been in, from one end of the midwest to the other. It was nice. No, it was *great*. It was fantastic, it was beautiful. I wanted it. But as quickly as that burst was shot across my tongue, it stopped.

I opened my eyes, and looked up at him. He was smiling knowingly. He knew! God, he *knew* exactly what he was doing! What he'd just *done*... I wondered absentmindedly if he had ever tasted it, if some hot man had done this to *him* once upon a time? But I didn't care. I just knew he was enjoying pissing on and into *me*. That was fine. And he knew it.

"Here," he said, and once more gave me the bottle. "Take a nice one, and get *ready*."

I complied, taking as full and wild a hit as I dared. The steamy, shadowy room began to spin a bit, and suddenly his cockhead was at my mouth. I was kissing the tip of his dick and then...

It began to flow.

He opened his valve slowly, carefully, and his piss flowed into my mouth. I held the shaft of his cock lightly as my head swam in the rush of the poppers. The hot golden fluid coursed into my mouth, over my tongue and he spoke softly, distinctly, the order irresistible in its sublime obscenity, its power and beautiful perversity.

"Swallow. That's it. *Drink me*," he whispered.

I gulped, then swallowed, then sucked. I suckled and nursed. I drank from the font of Dean's goodness. He pissed and pissed, and I took it till I thought I would pass out from lack of breath. And I drank.

"*Drink me*," he whispered again, as I drank. I was drinking his *piss!* I was drinking *him*! Fuck! It was awesome, stupendous and spiritual.

Once more, he knew exactly where my endurance was, and relented. I gasped for air, then leaned back once more.

"Oh my god Dean! Oh my god..." I didn't even know what to say. I couldn't say *That's nice*; but it was. I couldn't say *Thank you*; yet I was immensely, unbelievably grateful. I couldn't say *Give me more*; but I wanted more, *more*... There just weren't words for this... Oh indeed I did. I wanted *more* of that!

"Yeah boy, it's OK. It's OK. You needed that, I know. You can have more. Want the poppers?" I nodded, he handed them to me. Slowly I again hit the bottle, deeply, then again. And again. I stroked my hand up the inside of his hairy thigh, then cupped his balls in my hand. His manhood pointed out at me, the slit glowing, seeming to invite me, telling me of what it held. His juices. Cum. Manly fluid.

Piss.

It offered, it promised, it beckoned. I leaned forward and again kissed the tip of that beautiful cock. My lips lightly encircled his corona and Dean took the poppers from me and hit slowly himself. Then, cupping his balls gently as I let my eyes close, I waited in the rush of hot water, steam and poppers. Silently wishing, hoping, begging for it... Waiting... Pleading... *Hoping...*

And then, slowly, again he opened. The fluid started and I was receiving his piss.

Piss.

Oh God. I savored it as much as I could, letting that golden nectar flow across my tongue, to the back of my throat, then swallowed. Dean leaned slightly backward. He pushed his hips forward as he drained, flowed and pissed for me.

He pissed for me, with me... In me. On me. Dean's wonderful, magnificent cock pissed around me, to me. I wanted to use every preposition in the language, and let it describe how I was receiving his *PISS*. Oh God, piss. I wanted it, more and more; already I *needed* it. I savored it, took it. *Loved* it. *Le Morte D'Arthur* sprang to mind.

"I did not know how empty was my soul...
...Until it was filled."

Oh fuck.

My cock was throbbing, rock hard and oozing. I took more from Dean, took it all. His flow slowed, then trickled off. I drank it down, and he was done. Empty.

He smiled at me and spoke softly.

"Good Boy; real good. You've never done that before, have you?"

"No man, I haven't. But... but... it's..."

"Yeah I know Boy, I know. You love it. You need it now, you'll always need it. But not just anyone's rank piss. You'll need *my* piss." He was proud, forceful and pompous. But I knew he was right. Already I knew that I'd have more, and fine fun with other men, taking piss, giving it... but none would ever compare to this moment. Ever. It was sacred, holy. I wanted the night to go on. And it would.

Dean pulled me up to my feet and held me again, then held my hard cock in his big hand. "There, let it flow..." he said. He gave me one more hit of the poppers and I relaxed, leaning backward onto his furry chest, his arms around me, and my cock opened up to pour my piss in the shower. We let it splash around, on myself, up my chest, onto his hands. On the curtain, on the walls. Dean reached out and grabbed a paper cup from the counter, then held it low for me. I knew what he was suggesting, and once more the fear, the initial shock and revulsion came over me. Quickly though I got past it. *His* piss had been heavenly. Could my own be so much worse? I relaxed and pissed, and Dean caught a nice cupful, then lifted it up.

To my utter shock he put it to his own lips, then took a slow sip from it. He paused, then quickly leaned in and kissed me, spewing my own piss into my mouth. I slurped, I gulped and drank it, then we did it again. He turned me on to a whole new world of pure horny man-pleasure, PISS. I loved it. He could do anything he wanted to me... anything. Just as long as I could have his cock and his *Piss*.

I let myself drain, horny and hot. I sighed, turned to him and kissed. Then we rinsed off and got out of the shower. We towelled off, then went to lay on the bed and watch TV. We still had 6 full beers, and began to drink them slowly. Dean didn't want to get drunk, but I persuaded him to drink 4 of them... I wanted him to fill his bladder again, and he complied. Again his cock got hard, so he fucked me and spurted his cum up my ass. Then it was time for him to *Piss*. I couldn't wait.

He suggested new positions; first, he lay back on the bed, me down on him sucking. He warned me first.

"You have to control yourself real well here, you don't want it on the sheets or you gotta sleep in it." He chuckled a bit, then put his hand on my head, pushing me down to take his load. I was ready.

"I won't spill a drop, Dean."

"Boy, you call me *SIR*," he said.

"I won't spill a drop, *SIR*!" He stroked me lightly and let me drink him. I took his dickhead in my lips and again, I waited in anticipation, all but desperate for that precious second when he began, when he opened to me. I held him and sucked, and then it happened. He pissed, up, into me. I drank. I gulped and suckled, nursed. I didn't spill a drop.

Four more times that night I was fucked, four more loads of his hot cum were spurted up my ass. And four more times I drank his bladder dry. I knelt and drank him beside the bed; I lay on my back and let him straddle me; I took it however he suggested. It was almost 6:00 AM when he finally said he had to leave. I was saddened, but it was time. I knew he wasn't going to sweep me up off that bed, out of that flea-bag hotel and take me home. Nor did I really want that. But...

He'd showed me a new and wonderful aspect of manly sex. He taught me about Piss. I kissed him once more as I let him out the door. "Bye Dean... bye... *SIR!*" I whispered. He smiled, kissed me hard and deep, then winked as he plopped a note into my hand and slid out the door.

"G'bye Boy. Till next time. You'll get more Boy, when you need it. Call."

I watched him walk down the hall to the elevator and disappear behind the sliding door. I went back into the room and slipped into bed. My asshole ached, burned and twitched. My guts rumbled, and I let a full burp slide up my throat. Piss, it tasted like Dean's *PISS*! A piss burp! I laughed low and quietly at the beautiful obscenity of it, and savored once more the taste of his juices. I was fast asleep at 9:00 when Tim returned from his night with Jerry.

"So how was *your* night alone, Girl?" he sang. He was chipper, obviously still plenty doped-up from their partying.

"Well," I said, "It was OK. I found someone to spend some time with..."

"Oh do tell!" he said. But he wasn't really interested.

Furthermore, how could I ever explain it? There were no words that he would ever be able to relate to for what I had experienced, what I had become. The hell with Tim; Dean and I would keep that our secret. I was a piss drinker, a shower queen, a Piss Boy. I loved it.

Piss.

PISS.

I wanted to sleep, needed to rest. Tim was geeked up though and ready to keep going.

No doubt Jerry or one of his pals had a connection and gave Tim some go-go powder. I didn't like the stuff he had, but whenever we were on these forays I wound up stoned, drunk and strung out. I wasn't ready for this crap.

"GIRLFRIEND! You've gotta get some _verve_ here! Time to sparkle! *Sparkle, Neely, Sparkle*!" he sang. "We need to get some grub and head OUT girl! The MINDY CITY is waiting for you!" He swished around the room, throwing clothes this way and that, getting got-up again. I laid on the bed, my head swimming and my asshole throbbing. *Dean, oh god give me Dean!* Make this faggot quit screaming and give me Dean's hot dick up my ass! Fuck!

I rolled over and moaned. "Goddam it, '*Mindy*'! I've been up all fucking night! He just left a little while before YOU came in..."

"Well dear, I've been 'up' all night too. All fucking night. All night fucking. Whatever. Jerry had some of his... *friends*... join us. Was quite the party."

"Oh? And what, or better, WHO, pray tell, was the object of this party?"

"Who the hell do you think? *ME!*" He twirled around and took a bow. "Jerry was first, then Glen, then Tom and Stevie, then Mike... shall I continue?"

I giggled; I sure wasn't put off by the idea. I pictured myself in the center of that group. Jerry was hot and hung, I'd met Glen and he was fine too. The others I didn't know. But somehow I never was able to get myself into those situations. Tim could sniff them out across a mile-wide cocktail lounge packed with smoke and disco lights, pick up a high roller for free drinks and dope, take on 4 or 5 or more hot men, fuck his brains out and still find his way home by sun-up. He laughed too, then must've decided he needed my company for the day after all.

"Well shit girlfriend, HERE!" He put a glass plate on the dresser top and opened a tiny baggie. He laid out 4 lines of white powder and prepped them with the blade. "I only need a little one; you do these up and GET YOURSELF TOGETHER, BITCH!"

I got up, sighed, and threw on some clothes. He'd left a rolled $20 bill after his snort and I picked it up. I took one line, then a second. Tim pretended not to notice as I slipped the bill into my pocket. This was his trip, his deal, at least for the first couple days; this and another on the dresser top was my 'allowance.' I did not like being beholden to him for anything, but he'd convinced me to come to Chicago with the stipulation he would provide the basics. I knew he'd live up to those basics, but that was it.

He chose some of his usual flashy, clingy clothes; way too sleek for 9:00 AM I thought, but what the hell did I know? He was able to get by, get over on everyone. Maybe that was part of it? I got moving as the snort pepped me up and dressed in gay casual. Tight jeans, nice shirt, a navy blue waist-jacket; and of course my favorite jockstrap. I'd be fine.

"Damn bitch, I'm not waiting all goddam morning for you. I'll meet you downstairs. Find me in Carton's." He turned to go to the door.

"BULLSHIT, you hold your fucking horses, I'm almost ready." We hadn't even gotten out the door and he was giving me crap; he could ditch me later if he had plans. He complied, and within 3 minutes we were seated in the deli. He ordered a sandwich, I chose the same item. We ate quickly; obviously he had ideas about the day's events.

The bill was presented.

"Well here girl, yours is $3.12."

"What? You pay that fucking thing." He huffed a bit, but didn't bitch. We left the deli and headed around Rush Street. A highway caution sign marked the entrance to a basement lounge. 'MEN WORKING,' it said. I was curious.

"Oh that's the Getting Loaded Zone," he said. "The leather queens like that place." It wasn't until he punned the name that I noticed the discreet sign: *Loading Zone*. I knew a bit about leathermen, but had had almost no exposure. Tim was unusually reticent around them, which I liked. Too male, too macho. He liked fashion, salons, make-up, faggy crap. I liked garages, gyms, jockstraps... and leather. And now, I had discovered, I liked piss. The memory of that first rush of piss onto my tongue as I kissed the tip of Dean's cock flashed through my mind. God... oh god. I flexed my belly and burped again, tiny burp. But yes, I could still taste it a tiny bit. Piss. I <u>willed</u> myself to taste it.

"Hmmmm..." I mused. "Maybe we can try that bar later?" Tim was evasive and noncommittal; I dropped it and asked, "By the way, where are we headed now?"

"To Lila's! She's right here on Oak you know... you'll *love* it. Tenth floor apartment and all." We continued up the street and soon approached a large townhouse-style apartment building. Grand, elegant, almost rococo in the decor and flash. Tim pressed a button beside the door and quickly we heard the buzzer opening the lock. Upstairs, Lila Marks was holding court in her living room, 3 screamers and 2 dykes in attendance when we arrived. They mock-toasted us with mimosas as Lila made introductions.

I'd met Paulie and Dave; John was a new one. Carlene and Darlene (no shit, and they were neither related nor lovers) sat on the divan on the other side. We greeted all around, then sat. Dave looked me up and down.

"My but aren't YOU the butch one?" he cooed. I wasn't sure if he was serious or insulting me. I didn't care; he'd last about 48 seconds at the Interchange, and he wasn't getting anywhere near my dick. I snorted something noncommittal in reply and accepted a drink from Lila's tray. I sipped: orange juice and cheap champagne. WAKE UP! Gagg gagg gagg...

The talk centered on some upcoming fashion spread in a local magazine. Not exactly New York, but it sure wasn't Minneapolis either. Tim LaRoque was oohing and aahing as Lila assured him of a _full body shot_ in the issue. The other 'models' were disdainful, having a bit more _arrivé_ to their portfolios. Dave and John excused themselves, we all knew they were going to snort. I leaned back on the divan, wishing I could have some too. As if reading my mind, Lila glanced at me and nodded her head toward the hallway where the boys had gone. I rose and followed them.

They had powder lined up on a mirror tile. Who knew where that thing had come from? Nasty rough edges told me it did not belong in Lila's beautifully refined environs. Dave bent over the vanity of the guest bathroom, a wide, sordid affair of fake marble and 'gold-tone' hardware and garish towels. You could easily fit eight people in the dang bathroom at once; and it wasn't unlikely there often were multiple users of the bathroom at her gatherings. He took his two long, thick lines, and handed a rolled up bill to John. He did likewise, then it was my turn.

Dave was whispering about someone, something deep and important; his limited vocabulary made it tough for him to punctuate his thoughts. Every other word was some declension or conjugation of 'fuck,' 'fucker' or 'fucking.' But it seemed that Dave had gotten his panties in a wad over one of the other agency queens, and he needed John to listen to the whole torrid account. Which for me meant they got their lines and handed me the rolled-up bill just as Tim had done, and scooted back out into the hallway lest I hear something juicy. Like I would ever know, care about or repeat any of the gossip of their 'modeling.' I leaned down to snort, taking my first line very slowly; by the time I was ready for the second, they were gone.

I stood and sniffed, adjusting my nostril, and left 4-5 large lines on the plate. But I picked up the small baggie they'd left on the vanity, and tucked it into my shirt pocket. The bill, still rolled, I shoved into my pants pocket; they had plenty more. I went back out to the 'court-room.' Lila smirked at me; at least she liked me.

"Better?" she asked, and I nodded as Tim was gesticulating about how he was going to have his hair 'feathered' and fluffed for his next shoot. Longish and parted in the center, the sections from the top halfway down his head formed his 'wings.' Very 70's, very disco... He'd tried to get me to emulate the style; he expected all his friends to emulate him in everything. I rarely did.

Lila's guests were grouping off in cliques as a few more had arrived. She expected to be in the center of the room, the center of attention, but side-bar conferences which would then be summarized for the Court were *de rigeur*. I kept to myself for most of it, and engaged Lila in a discussion about Halston versus Calvin Klein. At least I knew what was current... she enjoyed it. None of her coterie had anywhere near the education I did; it was refreshing for her. But quickly she needed to get back into the twists and turns of her protégé's soap-opera lives. She simply turned away from what we had been talking about and focused on another person. I was dismissed.

I didn't mind at all. I'd put in my appearance with Tim, we had a couple free cocktails and hors d'oeuvres, I got some materials and cash from it too (I still wasn't sure how much, but it wasn't a single, I knew that much.) I began to get restless as Lila was talking about having the guys make up some *fa-hee-ta's*. I'd never heard of it before, but I wasn't interested in fajitas anyhow.

Tim was already pawing at one of the newcomers, a dead-ringer for The Marlboro Man. He was tall, masculine and rugged-looking, but his open shirt showed a smooth, a shaved or waxed chest. His shaped, plucked eyebrows, immaculately buffed nails and (gawd, spare me...) *'bronzer'* made him look ready for a night on the town, though it was now barely past 2:00. I called it *'make-up,'* plain and simple. Conrad obviously possessed consummate skill in applying his own; Tim would no doubt pick up new and important insights from 'her'... fuck it.

Making discreet good-byes, I thanked Lila, made tentative plans about meeting back up with Tim (hours, days later; who knew?) and quietly excused myself. Gathering my jacket from the hall tree, I stopped long enough to copy the number from the slip on the face of the Western-Electric desk phone.

Lila came to the hall to see me out. She offered me several bills, which I accepted. "Here, Tim is going to be busy for at least a couple days. You might need this." I thanked her again.

There was a sudden burst of group laughter in the main room. She quickly returned to her place and began to oversee the action. Her voice sailed above the others.

"Oh Conrad! Show us *tha-yatt* again!" and I could see him posing in the center of it all. *Marlboro* my ass; how about a photo-shoot for *The Modess Man?* I call's 'em like I see's 'em... But the sudden chaos covered my exit. I was quickly out of the fashion-show and into the hall.

ON THE TOWN

I got down the hallway. As I was waiting for the elevator, one of Lila's neighbors walked past, heading to the trash chute. He sized me up, nodded and spoke.

"You escaping the orgy?"

I snickered and answered, "Yeah, I can only take so much you know?" He heartily agreed. Straight guy, he was not fond of Lila and her entourage. Tim had mentioned him to me; the nasty neighbor Nick. I surmised there was nothing wrong with Nick except he didn't care for screaming faggots and didn't like the bumping thumping disco coming from Lila's apartment from 4:00 PM Friday until 7:00 AM Monday every goddam weekend. And the 'boys' she had coming and going at all hours of the night...

"I'm Matt Schiffmann," I offered. He shook my hand and replied.

"Nick Stoddard." Then he huffed and spoke again. "You shouldn't be around those assholes, get yourself a life." I thought it was awfully critical and personal of him; but he _was_ right. I nodded as he stood tall and handsome at the chute door.

"Well... I'm not one of her stable, and I'm not in the 'business.' Besides, I much more like the company of _men_, real men. Not pretty-boys in fuckin' make-up." He laughed outright at that, his thick moustache twitching. He blue eyes were clear, sharp. Those eyes missed very little...

"Hey, if _you're_ gay, maybe so am I!" I laughed along with him, but didn't let the idea go any farther. He wasn't, and he wouldn't be, and he was <u>not</u> interested in me, but I was glad at least I'd made a good impression on Nick. You never knew when you might need a neighbor, even someone else's. Tim never did understand that. The elevator arrived and we shook again. I watched Nick walking back to his apartment as the elevator doors closed. But still I wondered what it would be like in _Nick's_ huge hallway bathroom, kneeling to suck the hot piss from _him_...

Within minutes I was down on Oak Street, and heading back into it all. The wind hustled, howled and whipped: it was no joke, the Windy City. I decided to get some real food and went into the café on the corner. Its doorway at the apex of Rush and Oak Streets, they were busy from 10:00 until 10:00 every day, but it seemed in a lull right then. I went in and got a table immediately.

I had a burger and fries: usual fare. I took my time, sizing up the locals, checking out the tourists, spotting the homos and dykes. Styles were changing rapidly and suddenly it was OK, especially in New York and the 'Second City,' Chicago, to be flashy, stylish, and obviously homosexual. It was _not_ in Minneapolis or Eau Claire or Fargo; it was _not_ in the places I usually traveled and lived. I finished at the café and walked over to Lakeshore Drive to do a little window-shopping.

I was standing outside the glassed showcase window of a classy jeweler, a huge stone edifice with double security doors more apropos to a bank vault than a retail store, when a black sedan rolled past. The horn honked and I spotted Nick Stoddard cruising up the drive. I waved, then walked down 2 more blocks, then back into the district, or 'dick-strict.'

I'd killed some time; the sun was setting and it was rapidly becoming cold. I bundled in my jacket a bit more snugly and headed up the sidewalk.

Streetlamps twinkled and suddenly there was a road-work marker: *Men Working*. The LoadingZone. I paused, looked down the staircase into the bar. Music drifted up as two men approached me from the west. One tall and lank, his partner shorter and somewhat stocky. They wore dark clothing, then as they drew closer I could see the fabric. Leather.

Black leather, the tall guy in riding chaps and jacket, round toed boots and his keys on his right hip. The shorter man wore faded jeans, heavy black boots and a thick leather jacket. Hardware of zippers and chains festooned that jacket, and a thick, heavy cock ring on his left epaulet shone in the streetlight. They were awesome, beautiful, and their hyper-masculinity sent me. They nodded as they turned and headed down the steps, the tall one stopping to allow his man to precede him. I watched, taking a slow drag of my cigarette.

Again that black sedan cruised down the street. A Lincoln Town Car, as gleaming and shiny as the day it rolled out of Willow Run Assembly. It slowed, stopped right in front of me and the driver's window slid down. Nick Stoddard again. He called out, "Yeah Matt, now *that's* where you belong!" I smiled as I stepped up to talk to him.

"Man, I've never seen leather like that... but I *like* it."

He agreed. "If I was ever going to go out with another guy, buddy, it would be one of these men. But you're not ready for the Zone in that stuff... get you some good jeans and a biker jacket, get rid of that country-club crap you're wearing." I looked wistfully back at the stairwell.

"I don't have any leather," I said softly. "I guess I'll have to get some real soon. Maybe once I get back to Minneapolis..."

"Shit, you're not going to find what you need in *Minnesota*! Get in." Curious, I went around to the passenger side and got in. He lurched the car up the street the 2 blocks to his (and Lila's) building, and swung into a parking slot on the street. Some men have all the luck; if I'd tried to park in this district, I'd've driven around the building eight times, and then had to park in Naperville. We got out.

"Come on," he said, and we headed up to his floor. Exiting the elevator, we could hear the booming bass of Lila's stereo reverberating down the hallway. He shook his head disdainfully. "Rude," he said, "Just plain rude," as he pulled keys from his coat.

Opening his door, he motioned me in and closed it behind us. The hallway was dark, with heavy wood panelling and beautiful furnishings. The doorway to his oversized bathroom was open, a dim light indicating the seductive recess within. I paused; Nick walked swiftly into the living room. "Come in here buddy," he said. I followed.

He threw his coat onto the couch and headed through his dining room and into the bedroom. I heard him slide a closet door, then drawers, smacking things open and closed. A minute later he returned, a mass of black leather goods in his arms. "Here, try these."

He presented me with a rather plain but well-worn motorcycle-style jacket. I took off my blue velvet waist-jacket and slipped it on. Cool and dark, smooth and luxurious, it reeked of leather and oil. It was fantastic. I felt my dick jump in anticipation. "*Oooh*," I said lightly, not having words. I noticed a walnut plaque on the wall, 'Harley Davidson' something-or-other. Nick smiled and offered more. He pawed through a bundle of denim, finding a pair of Levi's with buttons on the fly. Worn and soft, they smelled of a man, someone...

"Get those clothes off," he told me, and I quickly complied. Nick unashamedly checked me out as I stripped. He tossed the jeans onto the couch, then sorted through a mass of leather items, separating his choices for me from the rest. Soon a stack of treasures awaited me.

"What size shoes you take?" he asked.

"Ten, but wide," I answered. I was down to my jockstrap; I enjoyed him looking me over.

"Perfect! Here." A pair of tall boots with straps on the ankles was presented. In moments I had dressed in the gear he offered. Those snug jeans and a belt, a dark blue T-shirt and a checked flannel work shirt-- a lumberjack shirt. I became something new, fascinating. I tried the boots. Having been broken in by someone else, they were a bit uncomfortable at first, but my feet readily fit. Next he had me slip on a pair of leather chaps. The knees were cracked and a bit rough, but the zippers were intact. A leather cap completed the ensemble, and Nick looked me up and down.

"There! You look _fine_." He smiled. "I've had that stuff for years; I'm not into riding anymore, and you need it. Good." I was all but overwhelmed.

"_Now_ you're ready for The LoadingZone!" he laughed.

"Man, thanks! I don't know why you'd do this... you just met me..." I forced myself to speak, my voice low, almost a whisper I was so awed. I was afraid I might actually cry, and could barely force myself to look up at him.

Nick reached over to me, taking my shoulder firmly. He smiled, but spoke low as well, softly, reassuringly. I'm certain he knew what a moment it was for me, and not only let me revel in it, but was enjoying it himself. He knew what this would mean to me, to my life.

"Well, you need it, that's all. Besides, I got a brother who's gay. I'm not. And I'd just rather see you go with the _men_, and not the pussy-boys that hang out with that stupid bitch next door. Fag-hag..."

I laughed; that was a great phrase, and said it all. He went back to his room to change himself. I could just glimpse through the crack at the door jamb as he undressed, his body furry and muscled. He emerged a minute later, in snug jeans and his own leather jacket. He was a sight, no doubt. He was beautiful. Again I imagined what he would look like with his pants open, his piss pouring into my mouth... I forced the idea back down, away. Just thinking about this neat guy in such terms was an insult, to us both.

"OK then; let's get you back to the pub. Get you ready for your grand entrance!" I smiled and began to gather up my shoes and jacket, but he stopped me. "Leave that; you can't tote that shit around all night. Come back and get it later." I transferred everything from my pockets into the new duds.

We went back to the street level, and I headed toward the car. He stopped me. "No, let's walk. I'll never get that spot again." We walked and he told me of his baby brother, Alan. Nick obviously had loved him dearly, had fixed him up with guys and taken care of him. But Nick hadn't been there when Alan met up with some rowdy toughs at a drive-in movie theater. They'd beaten him into unconsciousness and left him in the men's room. Alan had died 9 days later. The thugs were never arrested or charged with anything, and a year or two later were probably still beating up queers.

"He never would've come on to a stranger. They just figured he was a fag and killed him. He was twenty-eight." Nick was wistful, angry still, the pain enduring. "But he liked men, no doubt about that..." We were at the stairs to the Zone

"Come on Matt! I'll get you a beer."

We descended and entered the dark cavern within. The smoke was dense, unbelievable. Cigar smoke swirled atop cigarettes, mixed with pipe smoke and candles. The reek of marijuana wafted past... someone actually smoking dope in a public tavern! This was incredible! A twangy country song was blasting from the juke-box. Men in leather, denim and flannel mixed and talked, leaning backwards on the bar. They stood along the side walls and danced together on the wooden floor, pawing and kissing and embracing. Peanut shells carpeted the carpet, big bowls of nuts and chips sat along the bar. God, it was heaven! Nick smiled, grabbed me by the shoulder and lead me to a bar stool.

We sat and ordered: two long-neck beers. Nick paid the barman and we looked around. A 50-ish, solidly-built man with a thick, <u>thick</u> beard and moustache came up to us. "Hey Nick! Who's this?"

Nick introduced us; the guy was fine. His leather vest sported literally dozens of brightly colored patches and insignia: Bike clubs, riding events, rodeos... it was impressive. "This is my new lil' brother, Matt. Hey Matt, Tony." I smiled, shook hands. God-*damn* was his grip strong! You wouldn't want to be on this guy's bad side I quickly surmised. We chatted a bit; Tony was not impressed with me at all. But he was decent to me.

Nick finished his beer and made ready to leave. He tossed a $20 bill onto the bar and said, "Have a few on me there, Matt. Be careful." I nodded that I would and thanked him deeply. My leather gear wafted heady scent around me... I'd not forget this seminal event, ever.

"I need you to come to me when you're ready to buy your first Harley," he said, and stroked my shoulder firmly. With a smile and a wave, he went to the door, to the stairs. Twice, leather-clad men stopped him before he could exit. They smiled and talked; obviously they'd bought a Harley or two from him. I watched with a profound sense of gratitude as he left, heading up the stairs and out into the night. He would've made someone a fine lover, partner, friend. I never saw him (or my old clothes) again.

––––––––––––

I sat alone for a bit, just watching the beautiful scene, the masculine, furry men dancing, pawing, kissing and playing with one another. I smiled and made eye contact with a few, but none came to talk to me. My demeanor wasn't adapted to this milieu as yet; the only experiences I'd had in gay bars were limited to discos and twinkie-boy crap. I'd always known it could be otherwise, but hadn't mastered the art. Well shit, I actually did pretty goddam well for 18. My instincts leaned to this kind of action, not the faggy bullshit Tim was into.

After a bit, a leather-clad young man at last approached me. He wore a vest hanging open over a lightly hairy chest, no shirt, jeans with chaps and a studded belt. A kind of leather cop-hat sat atop his head. He sported a nice beard and a leather strap with a buckle around his upper right arm. I figured it must be equivalent to the hankies, keys and such. Right bottom, left top... a quartet of bandannas stuck up from his right rear pocket. There were navy blue, yellow, red and dark green. Blue I knew; yellow I surmised could only mean piss. The others were new to me.

He smiled and spoke. "Hey, we haven't seen you in here before. Daddy said I should come say hi, see what's up." He flicked his head toward the side rail; a furry grizzled man smiled at us and lifted his beer bottle. "That's my Daddy, Warren. I'm Carl." I introduced myself and we chatted a bit. I explained my newness to the leather scene and how fascinated I was with all of it. I asked about his colors.

"Yup, yellow means I take Daddy's piss; blue I get fucked. The red means he fists me and hunter green means I got a Daddy; I'm his Boy." Suddenly the fact of Dean giving me his piss and calling me 'Boy' made sense. He was a *Daddy*. Daddy-Dean. Woof!

I had to ask about fisting. The word indicated something WILD, intense, frightening and horrible. Could it be? Indeed, Carl told me about Crisco and their sling; Warren actually shoved his whole forearm up this boy's asshole and explored him from inside out. It scared the hell out of me just to think about it. But I told him about my recent piss-introduction. He smiled.

"Oh yes, I always knew I wanted to drink piss, take it right from the hose! Daddy loves to feed me, and shares me with his friends. I'm gonna be in the trough tonight, my first time."

"What? *Trough*?"

"Yeah, there's a piss-trough in the back room, over there." He pointed to a nondescript door on the far wall, at the back of the lounge. "He's got about eight guys lined up to piss for me all at once. I can't wait!" It sounded wild, horny and obscene. I asked if I could join them.

"I'll ask Daddy, but I'm sure he won't mind. *'The more, the merrier!'* Let me go get him."

Warren joined us directly, smiling and joking. He readily agreed to let me watch the piss-scene they had planned. He pointed out several of his buddies, men who would be taking part in the action. Dave and Mike, Marky and Jeff, Holden and Halsted, others. He told Carl to go talk to another 'boy' at the back wall and then began to explore what I was all about.

"You got a Daddy?" he asked.

"Um, no... I'm here alone. No partner." He smiled a bit and clarified.

"I mean, you got someone to feed and fuck you regular? Fist you and give you what you need?" I stiffened.

"I only took piss for the first time *last night,* Warren. And nobody is <u>ever</u> going to put his fist up my asshole. I don't mind getting fucked, but *I* am going to be shoving my cock up my 'partner's' ass when and if I ever have a relationship."

"Whoa!" he grinned. "A hot little topman huh?" I nodded.

"I guess <u>so</u>, man." I refused to call him 'Sir.'

He ran his hand up my leg and groped my genitals firmly, feeling me up simply as a matter of getting acquainted. "Yeah, OK, you got the kahunas for it, cool. And here I thought maybe you were another little pig-boy in from CowTown looking for a Daddy," he chuckled.

"I thought you wanted to join Carl in the trough... guess you'll be with the men on the side, huh? Good! It'll be hot to watch you piss."

I didn't tell him I hadn't thought about actually taking part in it all; but why not? I ordered another beer for each of us, and Warren reached for his wallet. I stopped him, instinctively knowing the power-play of who pays. I'd been carefully observing my dad and his bank associates for years. "This one's on *me*," I said firmly. He didn't protest, glibly allowing me the upper hand.

"Yes SIR!" he said, and I was filled with a kind of horny rush at being elevated from 'pig-boy' to 'SIR' so quickly, and he wasn't being entirely sarcastic. I had a lot to learn, but I was glad that so far at least I hadn't made any serious social mistakes in this new environment.

I pulled the money from my pocket and finally saw what I had with me. The grubby bill from snorting at Lila's was in fact a $100; I was just about floored. The wad she'd handed me leaving was another hundred. With Tim's 'allowance' and what I'd brought along, I had well over $300 on me. I had to separate it, put most into my back pocket and left 60 for fun. It still pissed me off that the Nixon administration had pulled all the large bills out of circulation. I had a $500 bill put away at home, but hadn't seen another $500 or $1000 bill since 1973.

Warren sat with me to drink his beer. A few of the other LoadingZone regulars came up to talk to him, to us. He introduced me to each of them. Marky J asked me how I knew Nick. I quickly explained, saying I knew Lila from a family member. He only knew about her noise, and nothing about her coterie of fag-boys. I didn't elaborate. They left me after a while, and I circulated a bit, talking to guys and checking out the scene from different angles. Carl caught me on one of my passes.

"The boys back there have a little white if you're into it. I'm sure they'd share with you. But once you get known here a bit better you'll have to provide some too." I had him introduce me, and going into one (of several, I found) of the back rooms I had a couple good ones. I hadn't realized how draggy I had been till it perked me up. I was ready to play.

The night wound on, and it was nearly midnight when Warren and Marky came to get me. "Hey, it's almost time to give Carl his little party," he told me. "Slug down another beer or two, then come back with us. Carl and Donny are getting it all ready." Donny was another Boy; I'm not sure who was his Daddy and I didn't really care.

I ordered 2 more beers and chugged the first one down. My belly was full, pressure in my gut and in the tight, faded 501's Nick had given me told me I'd be more than ready to offer my part. Taking the nearly empty bottle and the full one beside it, I made my way to the back wall. The door to the dark, secret room was open. There was a low hubbub around it, the tension quite palpable. Bar regulars knew something heavy was about to take place; and those who were involved gathered and quickly went inside. I sidled up to Warren and he motioned me in. I found a barstool along the wall to the right and perched. A wooden ledge, 'bar,' ran along the whole wall. I parked my beers and checked out the arrangements.

The room was about 30 x 25 feet, substantial. Minimal furnishings were present, the main feature being a large wooden 'X' on the far wall. The hardware glinted: two chains hung from the upper segments, D-rings, mounting buckles, more. I'd never heard anything about this kind of kink, but the purpose and function of St. Andrew's Cross was patently obvious. I'd had fantasies involving sexual bondage and domination since grade school, as both dom and sub. And I'd known even then I was not alone in thinking this stuff up. But now here were all those fantasies and then some... in reality. And men... nothing but men in the fantasy _and_ the reality. Girls didn't exist. It was hot.

The wall to the left of the doorway featured a regular white bathtub, a fairly well-finished plywood deck housing and skirting around it. I didn't see any spigots or plumbing; apparently they didn't need water for 'watersports.' Carl was standing near it when Warren closed the door and locked it. We were ready.

Warren walked back to the edge of the tub and stood center. He wrapped his arm around Carl and began to make an introduction. He had a large voice, commanding and clear. The room was quiet instantly when he began to speak.

"Hey guys! Listen up! *Friends, Romans, countrymen! Lend me your ears!*" We laughed a bit, Carl grinned. "Tonight is a special event as you know. Just 3 weeks ago I took Carl to be my Boy and he's shown himself to be damn fine, capable and more than willing not only please, but to do whatever it takes to please me." He coughed. "As we sometimes do, I've let the worthies among you sample a bit of his ahem... talents. And he's made me downright proud. But..." (Carl took one step forward, hands behind his back, glorified in his Daddy's praise and ready to show him correct in all respects.)

"He's also shown a great aptitude for piss. I love to give it to him, and have hardly flushed any since this Boy has come to serve me." Again some chuckling at this, but serious, we all knew he wasn't kidding. "In fact, I don't seem to be able to give the piss-boy enough!" We roared aloud.

"Everyone here knows what we intend to do, to satisfy this Boy and have a good time. Let him wallow in it, oink and grunt and take it all. This boy needs to be hosed down, filled up and show us what he's made of. Carl... strip."

The men stepped back and Carl, in the center, quickly but VERY neatly and efficiently removed his clothing. Leather, denim, boots, socks, accessories, down to a close-fitting beautiful jockstrap. His lightly furred chest was well-formed, lined from gym-work; his legs strong and his butt 2 orbs of wondrous, firm boy-butt. If anyone could resist porking that ass, it would be a miracle on the order of the loaves and fishes. He then replaced his socks and tied on his boots. Warren removed his leather arm strap and knotted a yellow bandanna in its place. With a nod, Carl got into the tub and slowly knelt, looking at the men gathering close around him.

I stayed a bit back, on my high stool, to watch. But the thickening bulge in my own jockstrap forced me to stand up and straighten my stuff before it became truly painful. Warren motioned to 2 of the men, Marky J and another. Mark was a god, pure and simple, his own physique not matched in this gathering. About 32, he was 5'10 and perhaps 190 pounds of fine, refined muscle and lightly furred on his chest and fore-arms.

He wore frayed, ratty jeans beneath beautiful leather chaps. An open vest and no shirt revealed a body harness with straps and buckles. He was beautiful. He smiled beneath his horseshoe moustache, then unbuttoned, pulling the flaps of his 501's aside and showing his incredible man-meat and glorious chestnut-brown bush.

He waved, holding a long neck bottle of beer and stepped up to the edge of the tub. Carl grinned; what a piece to start on! Marky held his own cock a second, then with a grunt began to piss.

The stream was yellow, bright and golden, and Carl gave a little moan of pleasure and enjoyed as it splashed across his chest, down his body and dampened his jock. But that certainly was not what he was assigned to do, nor wanted to do. He leaned forward, his open mouth inviting Marky to explore. He did, quickly inserting that fine, hot meat into the thirsty boy's mouth and with subdued huffing and moaning began to feed him. Carl gulped and guzzled, drinking in rapt joy.

Others were already lining up to take their turns. Some began to hose him down, splashing piss on him while one or another fed his craving need. Quickly he was soaked, drenched in hot man-piss, while each in turn gave him their precious elixir to drink. Four, five... more. Warren looked over at me and motioned.

"You're not sittin' on the sidelines there Daddy... get over here and give my Boy his due." I smiled and got up, approaching the scene. My bulge was obvious, and being unknown till this night, the men were highly interested to see what I was carrying. They parted, making room for me to advance. I walked slowly up to the boy in the tub and unzipped slowly, then let my jeans fall halfway down my thighs. My jock bulged nicely, a good wet spot showing the ooze.

How does a greedy piss-boy _smile_ with someone's dick in his mouth, pouring hot, delicious man-piss into him? Carl did! You could see the greed and elation when I approached. I waited for the big burly Daddy pissing on and in him to finish, to be drained. His stream abated, he smiled and stepped back.

"Hey young 'un, HERE! Show us what you got!" There was general agreement to the idea and I tugged the side of the pouch open, letting the whole of my manly equipment flop out. My dick was more than half hard, and a string of precum strung itself from my piss-slit to the fabric of the jock. Holden or Halsted, whichever, was at my side with a lecherous gleam of desire watching that string, the precursor to a hot thick sweet load of cum, as he knew.

Warren gave me a slap on the shoulder as I advanced, saying, "Yeah that's it buddy! Woof, you got the stuff! Feed him!" Then he turned to the room in general. "This is Harley Nick's latest protégé; Nick said we should be good to Matt." They murmured in assent and greetings, and I was ready to perform.

I'd only pissed a little bit shortly after arriving. Since the seminal, life-changing meeting with Dean Cordell, I'd been holding my piss all day. Each time I felt I had to drain my bladder, I forced myself to hold it as long as I could. I'd pissed twice all day. I was full, almost painfully so. There was no 'stage fright' keeping me from loosening my valve and I let a solid, powerful jet of yellow piss fly onto Carl. I held my cock at the base and tightened, slowing the flow.

I gripped it fully, stopping myself as I'd often done as a kid, playing, experimenting, learning about myself. Then a quick release and the stream BLASTED forth again. Carl loved it, and motioned for me to come closer, closer... to let him take it. I leaned over the edge, my hand bracing on the back wall, one foot on the rim of the tub. Carl moaned lightly in pleasure and took me to the bush. I opened again and pissed for him, for the first time in my life feeding my juice to another man.

I didn't know how he could do it, at the time, but he pulled the head of my cock back into his tonsils and GULPED, taking not only my piss but half my dick down his gullet. I pissed on full-force, full throttle and he let it flow directly down his esophagus. I think I was pissing directly into his stomach, god was it hot! He closed his eyes and simply worshipped as the piss flowed and filled him. I pissed for a solid minute, maybe longer, giving him every last drop. I moaned in satisfaction and horny pleasure, now knowing, understanding the joy, the pure elation he must've felt to take the juice from so many fine, beautiful men at once. *Someday*, I thought... *someday*...

I finished and drew back, my cock now almost totally hard. The more I pissed the harder I'd gotten. It was nice; and the men yelled and cat-called their approval. "Yeah Daddy! Give it to him man! That's *hot*!" "Yeah buddy, give him that man-meat!" "Hell yeah Matt, that's some *piss*!" "Woof Daddy, show us that cock!" I smiled, and went back to my stool, looking for another beer. As if by telepathy, Marky J was at my side, and gave me a tall, cold Bud. I looked at him in *awe*... Jeezus, God made homos that fuckin' beautiful? *Et Te Deum laudamus propter se!* Goddam! I could hardly talk.

He was fine, congenial, and quickly put me at ease not only with himself but the whole scene. Until he smiled and I dropped my guard, I had had no idea how much tension I'd actually been under. The snorting hadn't helped. But I was still awake and going.

He shook my hand, made small talk, and let me stroke his body. I wanted to kiss him so badly, and again, he simply leaned in and gave me what I was craving. I wanted more... more from him. He smiled again, his light Southern twang sending peaceful jolts of fascinated electricity through me.

"We're going to a party after this you know... would you like to come along?" I readily agreed, but mentioned that I was an out-of-towner, I had no wheels. No worries; he'd take me. I had to add one thought though.

"Marky... I'd love to get into some action with you man," and he listened brightly, respectfully. "I know I'm not the kind of guy you probably like to meet up with, but I'd sure like..." He didn't let me finish.

"Matt, I _know_ I'll like being with you man. Give me some piss like you just gave that Boy, we'll get along fine. I got straps on both arms, you know." I hadn't known.

"Um, yeah COOL! Whatever you like Marky; but that goes double." He gave me a quizzical look.

"Feed me _your_ piss like _you_ just did, and the rest will take care of itself."

"DEAL!" he said, and we hardly noticed the rest of the action.

It was after 2:30 by the time the scene dissolved. Carl had drank the full piss-loads of 11 men. He'd taken seconds from some of them who'd recharged while he was in the first round. And he was coated, soaked with piss and sweat. We went back out into the main bar where the two bartenders were finishing their close-up. They grinned and cheered. "Yeah PISS BOY! ATTA BOY!" We were treated to one last beer even though the place was closed and locked, and the men began to trickle out to their respective destinations. Most would be going to Mickey's party, in the Marina City towers. Mark made sure I was ready.

"Yeah bud, you won't believe the place... I know just the most perfect spot where I can drink you; you drink me. Let's go man, I got a 12 pack in the car." I readily agreed.

With one more round of thanks to Warren and all the guys, and a good hug of congratulations to beaming, proud Carl, we were out of there.

CHICAGO NIGHTMARE

Mark and I arrived in the parking area at almost 3:00, the oddly-shaped building of the tower making the parking deck even windier than the street usually is. It was damn cold and just that much colder 5 stories above the Chicago River. Marky and I had drunk a beer in the car, readying ourselves. I was all but full again and I figured he was also. He lead me to the elevator and there was a definite purpose to his step: horny yeah, ready to play, yeah, wanting to party, yeah... but maybe about panicking in the physical need to _piss_ as well. That was fine with me.

We went up and I didn't even notice what floor we got off at; the 28th or maybe it was the 36th... who cared? He lead me down a quiet, beautiful hallway to an oaken door. We could hear music coming from within, but nothing like the _boomboomboom_ constantly echoing from Lila's. I briefly wondered about Tim and his evening. But again, who cared? We entered.

Several of the guys from the LoadingZone were already there, and I was introduced to the host. Mickey had not been out that evening, stuck at home with a busted-up ankle. "What's the fun of the Zone if I can't even move around, let alone DANTH?" he said. I almost laughed when he spoke. Solid and furry, leathered and fine looking, when he talked he had the softest, lispiest, _faggiest_ voice you could imagine. No wonder these men so often used feminine terms. Jeez! But I stifled it and he was pleased to see new blood... er, uh... meat... er, yeah, whatever.

 The furnishings were fantastic: an eclectic mix of heavy, fine traditional with hot chrome and steel, glass contemporary items. A fabulous ormolu chest graced the wall beside the entryway, which led into a huge living room filled with overstuffed couches, chairs and cabinetry along the walls. The collection of fine and even rare books and phono records in those shelves was amazing. The dining room opened from there, and a hallway leading into what had to be 3 or even 4 large bedrooms. Awesome.

We took our jackets into a bedroom and Marky hung them in a closet. "Don't leave your stuff out around these fuckers," he said. "Leather will disappear in a LoadingZone crowd faster than a snowball in hell." I was shocked; up until that second I'd been impressed only with the congeniality, the honesty and honor I'd perceived among the leathermen. Marky obviously thought otherwise. "Mickey wouldn't let anyone take anything from here. This is HIS room. It'll be locked in a little while."

It was only very dimly lit, but I could see the immense king-sized bed and its heaps of heavy comforters, pillows, dark upholstery and accessories. The bedside lamps were huge and brass, with cut crystal droplets dangling from their sides. They had to run $500 apiece. On a beside table was a collection of paraphernalia. Lube, poppers, more... dildos, instruments, steel things. I was amazed. It spoke of perversions and hot horny sex as yet untried, undreamt even. Concerning me and my fantasies, that said rather a lot.

Marky wasted no time though. "In here." He opened another door and snapped on the light in Mickey's bathroom. Brass fixtures and crystal gleamed and glimmered. The shower stall was of frosted glass and was fitted into the corner; very stylish and a great use of the limited space. It was large, easily 6' on the transverse side. He tugged the glass door open as I closed and locked the room door.

Pawing and groping, we undressed ourselves and each other in a hurry.

I was down to my jock, Mark had his jeans off and his cock stood out. A perfect seven inches, proportionately thick. His fantastic balls, perfect bush and furry belly were scented with mansweat and a hint of piss from the evening's action. I pressed myself to him, trying to kiss him. He slurped me once and brushed me away. In a moment he was in the shower stall and turned on the hot water. There were 3 shower heads, and the steam billowed quickly. I stepped in with him and he was on his knees, pulling at my jockstrap.

I swooned in the steam. Marky sucked on my dick and I could barely contain myself. Hard and oozing in a flash, I relaxed and let it flow. He grunted in urinary pleasure, gulping wildly. I let it rush totally, trying to overwhelm him. He grabbed my dick and controlled my flow, and took it all. It was great, beautiful and obscene, fine and hot. He drank and worshipped, his picture-perfect cock standing up to his navel, upright and hard as a rock.

On the pissing went; Marky continued to take it, gulping and letting his mouth fill, then gulping again. He let me pour my juice into his mouth, then squeezed his face tightly and shot a huge blast of my piss back out, around my cock and down my belly. My jock was soaked and fine; I would wear it proudly.

A minute, another... I pissed and he took it all. At last the flow slowed, I spurted a full blast, then a dribble. Holding myself tightly, I held back to give the last morsel in one pulse. He received it gladly and smiled. Then it was my turn.

We traded positions and just as quickly his pressurized bladder was hosing me down. I wallowed in it a moment, mixing his piss onto my own, wetting my body and sticky jockstrap. I guzzled, smelling his fine hair, his scent and sweat. I reached behind him and grabbed, kneaded his ass cheeks. He thrust forward a bit and ground his cock into me. I gulped and guzzled, slurped it down. It was watery, dreary and plain, but it came from his penis. It was man-piss, even if weak and beery.

Fondling his butt, he pulled his hips backward, lifting up and encouraging me to work his ass. His cheeks parted and I found his asshole. Hot and sticky, his crack was redolent of manly aroma, clean and inviting. I fingered the pucker and felt him flex and relax, tighten and relax and I pushed my fingertip into the tight sphincter as I continued to drink piss from him.

The stream poured on as I worked him, his body leaning slowly backward as he held his eyes closed. I swallowed again and again, feeling the foamy piss filling me, filling me. His feet were apart, his hard dick pointing deep into my throat. The piss flow began to staunch and I gulped once more, then forced two fingers into him with a hot shove. He grunted, spurt his last gob of thin urine into my mouth and pulled his cock away. He wanted the rest.

His hands went beneath my armpits and he pulled me to my feet. At last he gave me a full, delicious kiss, spicy and pungent of beer, piss and smoke. I wrapped my arms around him and held him tight, then he slowly pulled away and turned to the wall. He placed his hands on the tile, his feet apart and ass cheeks open, ready.

"Fuck me man, fuck me!" he said. He wanted no prep, no finesse. I spat a gob onto my hand and slicked up my hot hard cock. Already I was oozing, having needed to blow the load when Carl got me going back at the bar. With a deep hot shove I entered him, thrusting half my cock into him across the back of his prostate.

"Ughgghhhhh yeah fucker YEAH! That's it, hard man! Fuck me!" I grunted in reply, and worked him into position to take the full length of my 8" phallus. I adjusted my stance and shoved, thrusting to the hilt. Marky bellowed in pain and pleasure, wanting it all. I reached around to stroke his cock as I fucked.

My balls mashed against the beautiful flesh of his thigh and the sensations worked me. I mashed myself harder, fitting my cock into the welcoming hole as my balls snuggled between his thighs. In seconds I was ready to shoot.

"Yeah man YEAH! I'm gonna cum man, here it is... ughgggggggghhhhhhh yeah!"

"Fuck yeah man me too, here it cums!"

I stroked him and with a loud groan his cum shot across my hand and splattered on the wall. "Agggggh fuck yeah man, give it to me!" I pumped again, spurting the whole of my load into him in hot jolts, my balls aching in relief.

In merest seconds we had finished, and Marky leaned against the wall, pulling himself off my cock. I tried to hold myself in his hole, enjoying the sensations of his clenching, pulsating asshole ring, but he was done. He turned and gave me a pat on the shoulder, one quick kiss and said, "Yeah man, yeah! Hot fucker. Let's go get a beer."

And we were done.

We dressed quickly and returned to the main rooms. Others had gathered and there were now about 20-22 men present. Marky slid away from me in a flash, and joined a clique of leathered-up guys. They didn't pay attention to me, and I went to talk to Warren.

"So you got some of Marky J did ya? Hehehe." He smiled, knowingly. "Quite the little pig isn't he? You'd never think it, but he's a *sick* one. Give him piss?"

I nodded.

"Didja *fuck* him?"

I smiled again, "Yup sure did."

"Good."

Warren was just about totally smashed, Carl going about the room serving one and all as Mickey sat and held court, not unlike Lila's *soirée* (*matinée?*) hours and hours ago. I felt dizzy, drained and drunk myself. I'd need to sleep or something very soon. I wondered how I'd get back up to the hotel, since Marky was no longer in sight at all. I figured he'd gone on to round two for the night, of how many no one could say. I thought it was hot that whoever was next would be fucking into my load. Maybe I'd been fucking into someone else's sperm in his rectum? I didn't know.

I accepted a drink Carl offered, then joined some guys by the huge window above the river, looking out over the twinkling, cold city. They were friendly, buzzed and laughing. They passed me a flimsy cigarette and I took a hit.

The best (or worst, depending on perspective) herb I've <u>ever</u> encountered coursed through my brain and I gave it up. After a single toke I all but swooned, and headed for the bar in the dining room. The room spun, tilted, and I saw a grinning Warren standing behind the bar, a large chunk of polished onyx at least a foot across held 10-12 long heavy lines of white.

"Matt get over here man," he slurred, offering me a crystal snifter of god-knows-what. That was the last conscious glimpse of the party I remember.

A white cloud opened and slowly began to come into focus. Short white lines went sideways, right to left, about halfway across my field of vision. I was trying to figure out what the hell short, thick white lines could mean when my inner ear finally adjusted. The weird vertigo balanced and gravity returned. The lines went from right (floor) to left (up.) They were the fibers of the pale carpet. I tried to lift my head. Ouch.

I laid it back on the floor and waited a minute. Then I rolled over and tried to take stock of the situation. My nose hurt, thick and swollen. My mouth felt like a troop of Sumatran baboons had encamped and defecated in there for a month or so. My legs ached, my knees badly carpet-burned... I pulled myself to a sitting position. I was naked but for my strap. Uggh. I looked down, my genitals hanging beside the pouch of my jock. Sticky, gooey... and was that blood there too? I didn't know. I looked around.

The pale room was bathed in the soft light of early morning. There was no furniture in it at all; I had no idea this room existed. Clothing lay strewn about. I recognized my (Nick's) jeans and belt. I looked about me and then, I saw it. Her.

A woman lay on the floor about 4 feet away from me, naked but for her bra. Her saggy tit appeared to ooze and run out from under the thick fabric of the cup. I stared a moment, utterly horrified and shocked. She was motionless, comatose or as close to it as possible without brain damage... Or _with_ brain damage, the way I felt. A streak of blood marked her flabby belly.

"OH FOR FUCKIN' CHRIST SAKE _NO_! NOT _THAT!_" I thought, silently screaming within my throbbing skull. I examined myself a bit closer, there was hair in my mouth, in my _teeth_. Unbelievable. I wanted to go to the window, go through it. The river would be clean at least; goddam cold, and 36 stories down, but clean fresh water. That wouldn't be all bad.

My hand ran up my face, across my mouth and came back with crusted, all-but-dried blood. I looked back at the woman again... and almost vomited.

I began to pull myself to my feet, no, to my knees. I crawled about the room, sorting through the clothing and actually found all of mine. But my boots were not to be seen. I dressed as much as I could, in pain and disgust, horrified, and crawled to the door.

Before I got to the door, my hand slipped through something sticky, nasty and cold. I forced myself to look at it. Greasy, whitish and thick, brown streaks marked the puddle. Cum. From someone's asshole. Jesus. What next? I felt my own butt. No, I'd not been fucked. It wasn't mine... oh well then ok; that's different.

At last standing up and going into the hall, I was dumbfounded at the devastation. It was as if a cyclone had traversed the beautiful apartment. The mirror was broken, glass scattered down the carpet. I walked carefully, and managed to avoid sticking my feet in it. I got to the bathroom and was able to take a look at myself. I scratched at the blood on my face, on my nose... It was my own, THANK GOD. I knocked a gobby scab aside and a freshet of new blood ran slowly from my nostril. Ah, yes, let's have _another_ line, OK? Jesus fuckin' Christ...I let it bleed and adjusted my clothes.

I got out to the living room and wasn't really all that surprised to see bodies strewn about as were their clothing. Black leather, steel hardware, denim, flannel. (Oh cool, there's my boots.) Carl lay draped across a couch, his head lolling over the armrest. Damn. Warren was on the floor behind the bar, still. That fuckin' snifter taunted me, still holding some vile, powerful brown liquid. Bottles and ashtrays, butts were everywhere. I heard clinking and made my way into the kitchen. Two sorry-looking leathermen sat at the table, drinking coffee and smoking. They looked up.

"Ho, another one makes it back from the river Styx!" one said. The other looked confused.

"Styx? Fuck... I was _way_ farther down than that, baby. Coccytus..." The bearded survivor howled in laughter. His companion smacked him hard, trying to stop the noise. I was glad he did. "Who the hell are you guys?" They laughed again.

"I'm Don; this little fuck is Gerhard. We met last night Matt... And it's always nice to see when the literati make it through an evening at

Mickey's. That's not to be taken for granted." He laughed insanely. "The coffee is right there." I opened a couple cabinets and found a mug, and helped myself. God. They offered a few clues about how I'd gone down, and no, it hadn't been that bad. The hung-over Nazi with the headache said he'd seen me take one of the leather twins, Holden or Halsted (I wasn't the only one who couldn't remember which was which) into the back room, *"with definite purpose in mind."* Ah, OK. They were both fine; I guess whichever one I'd fucked had been happy too, he'd gone back out to report on it, and they hadn't seen me again. OK then, maybe the puddle of cum *was* mine, from Holden's ass? Hmmm...

I had a cup of coffee and the boys said they were going back to bed. There were four men in Mickey's bed at the moment, and others on the floor and the chaise. They were going back and maybe start a morning 7-way or something. Gerhard gagged on his own breath and left the room. I shrugged and Don left me as well. I finished my coffee and went to the living room.

I didn't exactly rifle coats and such, or strip the corpses of the dead, but I did scout the room for worthwhile things. I found a good quarter-ounce of someone's high-quality powder laying on the bar with my own cigarettes, a mashed pack of unfiltered Camels; and the remainder of that green shit from fuckin' Thailand. Or Hell, whichever. It didn't matter.

I tucked myself together then headed back to Mickey's room. Indeed, the heap of clothed, partly clothed and unclothed man-flesh in the bed was truly astounding. Five men (including Don,) lay twined together in the bed. Marky J was passed out buns-up at the foot of the bed, his furry ass slick with lube and semen. I was proud of myself, knowing mine was the first load of what was in him. The closet door was open, and once more I was amazed to find my goods were intact. I put my jacket on and grabbed my cap, glanced once more around the incredible wreckage of the magnificent home and made my way OUT.

The fuzz in my mouth and hair in my teeth made me think once more about going to the window at the end of the hall, there was a clean river down there... but I stepped into the elevator instead.

BACK TO SCHOOL

I got the hell out of Marina City, and I've never, ever been back.

Heading down the street, I was pleasantly surprised at the mild conditions that morning. Somehow during the night it had warmed considerably, rare for Chicago. I walked toward Union Station, intending to hail a cab back to the hotel, but the crap in my mouth, on my teeth, was making me nuts. I was all but in a panic needing to clean myself.

I'd not brushed my teeth at Mickey's, being programmed by childhood training about never using anyone else's toothbrush. Yeah right... I'd had my tongue up stranger's assholes, their cocks, piss and cum in my mouth, kissing and slurping their tongues, their faces, chests and appendages; but a plastic toothbrush was 'dirty.' Go figure. I looked for a store, a 7-11, a drug store, anything. It was Sunday.

I was in the heart of the second-largest city in the country, and there was nothing open. On I went, 4 blocks, 5... Nothing. FINALLY I came to a kind of downtown strip-mall. A Ben Franklin, a Kroger, a barber shop, Chinese food, key grinder and scissors sharpening... all closed. And Osco. The only thing open was the drug store, thank god. I headed across the parking lot and in. Locals and workers alike looked me up, down, all over; most backed away. I already had a pretty good idea of just how bad it looked, but the reactions of the shoppers that Sunday morning gave me convincing proof.

I'm sure they weren't exactly thrilled to see a wrecked leatherman stumbling through the store at 10:00 AM. I didn't care, and found the aisle with toothcare products. I grabbed the cheapest little kit I could find: some Colgate thing with a 'sample' of toothpaste and a blue brush. Perfect. There was no such thing as bottled water, and I hustled to the cooler and selected a bottle of Canada Dry club soda.

Heading to the check-out, a family of 4 pasted themselves backwards to the shelves of candy and snacks as I walked by, genuine fear in their eyes. I was astounded; the elder son had to be 16 or 17... for Christ's sake that little zit-ranch was at most 2 years younger than me, *if* that! I kept my eyes on the floor and got past them as quickly as I could.

I paid and got the hell out, back on the street. I walked away from the little mall and onto Michigan Avenue. In the doorway of yet another tightly-closed business, I stripped open my toothbrush and uncapped the paste. I prepared my utensils and threw the paper and sack into a trash barrel. With 2 quick steps I sat down on the curb and opened the soda. I brushed my teeth, rinsing in club soda and spitting gobs of my own mucous, Holden's pubic hair and endless cigarette smoke into the gutter.

At long last I felt human, like I could talk. I should've been disgusted beyond bounds, but I was past it. I rinsed again, then took a drink from the bottle. Tossing it into the barrel last, I stepped off the curb and into the street, waiting for the next cab. From 3 blocks away a white and blue Checker Marathon spotted me, and he was there in about 28 seconds. It wasn't exactly prime time for hacks in downtown Chicago, and he sure wanted the fare.

He was decent looking, about 25 or 26, a nicely trimmed beard and long brown hair. Blue eyes twinkled and he was more than ready for a leatherman to ride with him.

"Hey man," (*May-ann...*) "Heading out for fun?"

"Geez no... Trying to recover from all the fucking 'fun.' All I want is a hot shower and a pillow!" He laughed wildly, hurting my head.

"You got someplace to go? I can get you fixed up if you need...?" Damn, a come-on, and I was wrecked. He was even kind of cute, somewhat like Marky in a grubby way.

"Um, man... I'd take you in a second, but I gotta get to my room. Rush Street; the Maryland Hotel, OK?" He wasn't too disappointed, he'd find some cock that morning, I had no doubt. He hopped back into traffic and headed up Halsted (yeah, just like the leatherman.) It took a lot longer than I'd expected, I was damn glad I'd not had to walk. But finally we pulled up in front of Carton's, the deli in the front corner of the Maryland Hotel. I paid him, tipped him nicely and made to get out. He paused again.

"I only drive until 2:00," he said. "Maybe you'd like some company a little later?"

I smiled. "Wow, yeah. May-_be_... You have a number?"

"No man; I thought I could just come by..."

"Well, I'm not sure I'll be ready to play by 2:00; but I'm in 1806. Matt..." I extended my hand. He shook it and grinned. His teeth were not pretty.

"Norton." I grunted and opened the door. He added, "I'll just come up when I'm off shift."

"Man, call the hotel," I said snidely. "She'll put you through. Give me some warning, OK? The desk lady's not gonna like it if I got someone showing up I when I'm not even sure I'm gonna be alive!"

He wasn't happy with the idea, and glumly said, "Well... OK man..." (_May-ann..._) I got out and headed through the lobby past the aforementioned desk lady, Janice. She was a 50-ish, painted up, fat old street whore who'd finally settled into life in the Maryland. The regulars and residents lived on the 12th floor, and she was one of them. Her nasty, snarling, utterly hateful Chihuahua 'Rex' was standing on the counter behind her teller's wicket. The vile thing snarled and yapped as I waved and hustled past, into the elevator and upstairs.

The room was just as I'd left it, or so I thought, and I got undressed. I went into the bathroom to shower, but hadn't the energy. I wiped myself down with a wet cloth and headed to bed. I was out like a light, and slept until the ridiculously loud phone jangled me awake at 2:07. Norton was on the corner and wanted to come up, 'for a little while.'

I got up and tightened my cock ring.

He appeared at the door within 3 minutes and I answered naked. He was ready also, and was on his knees in a flash. I was hard again in seconds and he wrestled himself out of his clothes. He was a lot slimmer than Marky, but his cock was much bigger, fat and veiny. The head of it was a huge knob, disproportionate to the shaft, large as that was. I grabbed him and leaned down to suck him. He didn't want it and pulled back.

"Man, let's go over here," he said, pulling me by the hand. He flopped onto the bed, on his back, legs up and grabbed for the lube. He didn't want poppers and slapped grease onto his own asshole. "Come on man, gimme that cock!" His own dick lay on his belly, only half hard. I got into position.

"Yeah man, that's it, fuck me!" I grunted and shoved into him, giving him all of it. He barely moved, obviously highly experienced. My eight inches didn't phase him a bit, and I ground myself into the silken, soft and wide-open, welcoming flesh of his rectum. His eyes glazed over and he swivelled his hips, grinding me into his asshole. I began a hot hard fucking and stroked in and out fully, taking my time as I plumbed his depths.

He reached around to paw and grab my hips, my ass, and pulled me hard onto himself. With a groan, he bucked up and ground himself onto me hard, fully. His semi-flaccid dick pulsed a bit, and oozed his thick creamy cum onto his belly. "Ahhhh, ahhhh, ahhhhhhhh..." he moaned, and drooled a huge white load onto himself. My cock jumped and I drove in harder, but was nowhere near ready to cum.

"Man! Yeah man, oh yeah that's it!" He spurted a bit more, and he was finished. "Ummm, oh yeah man, thanks!" Norton said, and pulled himself back quickly. The way he twisted surprised me, but effectively knocked me out of the saddle. My cock fell away from his hole, and he was already getting up from the bed. "Wow, thanks!"

In seconds he had himself up and dressed, and headed for the door.

"Damn man, that was perfect. Take care!" With a click and slam, he was out the door and gone. I was amazed. He could rape a *topman*! He'd used me and left me high and dry; it was wild! My cock pulsed and wondered what had happened, hanging out in the chilly air. I went to the window and opened the drapes. Only then did I see the sticky brown sleaze smeared on my dick. Gawd... at least he hadn't wanted romance; I wouldn't have kissed him anyway. I went into the bathroom and finally took a full shower. I pondered the grimy street-fuck who'd just left. I wasn't quick enough on the uptake; I should've pushed him back on the bed and pissed on him, just out of contempt. Nah, piss was too nice. He didn't deserve it.

I enjoyed the hot water, the steam, and remembered Dean's presence with me only two days before. I relaxed and let my own stream flow in the hot water. Mmmmm, I wished he was here again. That reminded me, I had his phone number. Hehehe, yeah, ok... I needed some *real* fun! Norton, Schmorton; I cleaned myself and got dried off. I went to the bedside table and only then did I realize the drawer of the table was open. So were the drawers of the side dresser. Tim had cleared out.

I called Janice and asked her what the story was.

"Well fuck sugar, shit... I don't fuckin know. That little fuck didn't fuckin say fuckin shit to me. The fuckin rent is fuckin paid till fuckin Tuesday so what the fuck do you fuckin care anyhow? Fuckin stay. You fuckin need the fuckin linens changed and shit, or what the fuck should I fuckin do?" Her command of English astounded me. How *literate*! Her mommie and schoolteachers should've been right proud of her! She'd used some form of the word 'fuck' FIFTEEN TIMES in one statement.

———————

So Tim had cleared out, no doubt to get busy with his *full body shot* in the Chicago Fashion Parade. Maybe he'd get some action with Conrad, the Modess Man, too. So what? I had nothing to worry about for privacy, that was cool. I dug through my jeans' pockets and wallet. Dean... there it was. I got an outside line, and dialed. He answered on the 2nd ring.

"Yes?"

"Dean?" He recognized my voice, I was sure.

"*What*?"

"SIR?"

I could hear the smile in his voice. "Yes, Boy. What's up?"

"Sir, I was a bit lonely today. I wanted to invite you up to my suite in the Maryland Hotel, Sir. I'm... I'm..."

He chuckled. "You're what Boy? Tell me about it."

"Sir, I'm horny. My asshole is aching and I'm thirsty. I need you, Sir. I'm not just horny; I _need_ you, Sir"

"Oh, I know you do. I know son, and I'll be there to take care of you in about 40 minutes OK? I been expecting you to call. What took you so long?"

It wasn't an rhetorical question; he demanded an explanation. I drew in my breath and complied.

"Sir, I came to town with a friend, maybe you recall? But I had to accommodate his schedule. He's gone now, he won't trouble my plans any longer while I'm here. I mean, *our* plans, Sir." He was satisfied with that.

"I'm almost done with my second pot of coffee son; I don't know if I can hold it all." I sucked my breath in quickly.

"OH SIR! Please... *please* try..." He cut me off.

"I'm joshing you son. You get ready there, Boy, and I'll be up as quick as I can. Daddy'll be there to feed you. I'll hold it. You better be *real* thirsty Boy."

"Sir, I am. I am... I'll show you. I'm clean and ready, *thirsty*..."

He grunted, "Dismissed!" and hung up. I was already getting hard, and I went back to the bathroom to make sure I was prepared. I shaved, went to the toilet and showered again. I laid on my back in the tub and forced my ass up to the spigot, giving myself a quick enema. I was clean. I had just dried off and gotten into my jockstrap, and there was a knock at the door. Glancing at the clock I realized it had been 31 minutes. I was ready.

Opening the door, I wasn't a bit surprised to see Dean standing there with his cock pointing out the fly of his hot 501's. He stepped into the room and without a word I dropped to my knees. He touched the sides of my head lightly as I opened my mouth and he slid in. He buried ¾ of his cock into my mouth and I suckled, closing my eyes. He let me enjoy it for half a minute, then pulled back.

"You thirsty?" he asked, and I nodded. "Good; I'm full..." and he began to strip. Shoes, jeans, shirt... undershirt. He was down to...

His jockstrap. Oh God.

It had a standard Bike label, but this was special. It was blue, bright beautiful blue. A blue jock; I'd never seen anything but white. He filled it beautifully, his fat fine cock poking out the side.

I whispered softly, "Oh Sir... oh..." He smiled.

"Get to the tub son; Daddy's gotta go." I was glad he didn't want me to take him on the carpet. If he was that full, I wasn't sure I could actually handle all of it. He knew I couldn't, and didn't expect me to. We stepped quickly to the bathroom and I was in the tub in a matter of seconds, my bottle of poppers already open as Dean stepped up to the edge, but did not get in with me. I huffed deep and quick, 4 times on each side. It was whelming, and Dean took the bottle from me. I positioned myself to receive him; he sniffed quickly and moaned low and soft as he slid his cock between my lips.

"Yeah... yeah boy, that's it. Here you go..." and once more that heaven surrounded me. Dean and his hot cock pouring out his piss. His piss. Oh God.

Piss.

It rushed and filled my mouth in an instant, hot and golden. It was strong, thick. I swooned and swallowed, gulping slowly, letting it push the sides of my cheeks out, and then guzzled to catch up. Dean forced the stream hard and it overwhelmed me. Piss shot out my mouth around his dick and wet his balls, his bush. He thrust his cock into me harder.

"YEAH, take it boy, that's it. Drink me now, take it down. Daddy gotcha there huh? Hahaha, good. Good boy..." and he stroked the top of my head. I was gagging but held him tight, not wanting to lose any more than I absolutely had to. I reached up to caress and cradle his balls, the wet jock feeling fine and wonderful against my hand. He approved, and put his own hand down onto his basket. He wrapped his thick fingers around the base of his cock and tightened, slowing his stream.

Dean's glorious piss flowed slowly, fantastically, deliciously across my tongue. He knew how to feed me, there was no doubt. He let it run, then spurted to fill my mouth. I would slosh it around his cock, around my mouth, then swallow. A thin stream of the thick piss continued, but then he'd give another rush. On it went, that golden piss, that liquid silk, that holy man-juice. I was rapt, and for the third time in my life I drank piss; but this was again *his* piss. I drank in awe, in glory, in heavenly piss-pleasure.

My mind wandered, every expression for it going through my brain in seconds. Wizz, urine, pee... Wee-wee... none was any good at all. *Pee* was something that came out of a little girl's worthless, nasty slot. *Wizz* was something hairless adolescents told ball-field toidy jokes about. *Wee-wee* was something your mommie referred to, being too silly and polite to call it like it is. *Urine* had a nicer ring to it, and might be a useful term, in a kind of medicinal or clinical way. Like drinking piss from a doctor or something.

But this was PISS, nothing else. It was Dean's *Piss* and I was drinking him. I loved him for it. I drank him, gulping mouthful after mouthful of the sacred fluid. He squeezed the base of his cock and stopped the flow, then pulled out. "Here," he said. "Lean back, open your mouth *wide*..." I immediately did as he said. His huge tumescent penis flared, and a beautiful full stream shot out, perfectly aimed. He filled my mouth and I received it, held it. He stopped and spoke again.

"Don't swallow, hold that. HOLD it..." and motioned me to stand up. I rose and in a flash he'd embraced me, kissing and sucking his own piss from my mouth. He held it a moment, then spat it back to me. I held it, then swapped again. Piss ran down our chins and at last he spat it into my mouth and pushed me back a bit.

"Swallow it, yeah that's it Boy. Now... take another load," and pushed on my shoulders. I was back down in a second and sucked another full mouthful straight from the tip of his cock. His body was framed in the dark blue elastic, a vision of pure masculine honor and beauty. Again he pulled me up to shotgun back and forth. I was in ecstasy, and Dean loved it too. He fingered my asshole while he held and piss-kissed me. He crouched a bit, taking aim to shove 2 thick fingers into my hole, rough and fine. He wasn't going to pussy me; I was a man, a Man-Boy, and <u>liked</u> to be fucked. He was going to _fuck_ me too. There was no disputing that. He wrenched his right hand and painfully stretched my asshole, his left hand gripping my hip on the waistband of my strap. I ground onto his fingers and kissed him harder.

Once more he pushed me to my knees and this time shoved his cock to the back of my throat. "Drink now, take it... I don't _care_ if you choke, I'm going to finish!" he said, and pumped the last 20 seconds of his hot, hypnotic piss deep into my throat. It welled up, slid up into my sinuses. I let it go and drank as I could, and by sheer dint of _Will_ did not choke or pull back until he was done. He slowly pulled his penis from me and I coughed, then slurped the remnants of his load from my own nostrils. I was sated, and Daddy was drained. I rose.

Without ever having turned the water on, we got out of the shower and headed back into the bedroom. Once again Dean helped himself to the accessories and quickly had me on the bed, doggie-style, my ass hot and ready. He smacked the flat of his hand on my butt a few times, my cheek smarted from the impacts. With a smear of his fingers, my asshole was greased and I could only assume he slicked his phallus with the lube as well. I knew I had only a few seconds and twisted the lid from the poppers to get a massive hit before it was too late.

Dean grabbed the upper edge of my jockstrap and paused just long enough for me to get the full advantage of the rush, then...

He slammed that cock into me, fully.

My world exploded in overwhelming sensation. The taste of piss regurgitating under his assault flooded my mouth, but I choked it back. My asshole screamed, somehow I did not.

"Uggggggggh! Oh God SIR! YES!" I cried out, bucking back. I couldn't believe I tried to make him fuck me harder, wilder, but I did.

"Yeah Boy! GOOD BOY, that's it! Take it all, here you go, that's what you've needed!" He pulled back to the very edge of his corona and slammed into me a second time, harder, much harder and more painful than the first. Once again, the only thought I had was, *White Lightening*. The pain increased and I could hold back no longer.

"Oh God Sir! Oh god please, help me, damn it hurts!" He grabbed my hips and pulled me back harder, slamming into me again. He held his cock in me to the limit, then slowly drew back, drew out.

"Hmmmm... really?" he said. "Let's SEE about that!" I turned a bit, and looked back over my shoulder and saw the almost maniacal gleam in his eye. It scared me.

"Sir, please! Remember how you helped me? You looked in my eyes, and helped me to take it. Let me get a breath and take it properly, ok? Sir? Please?" His expression softened, and he relented. "*Help me...*"

"Yes, OK Boy, I understand. You need Daddy to help you accept, to open for this. On your back." I rolled over, grabbing the popper bottle again and reaching for the lube.

"Sure, more grease Boy, I'll get it." He took the lube as I hit the poppers again, hard and deep. Five, six full hits on each nostril and I swooned as he lifted my legs HIGH and open, then slowly pressed his cockhead to my hole.

With a slow, steady but inexorable force, he entered me totally once more. He leaned over me and looked into my eyes, and we spoke in unison.

"*It does NOT hurt!*" He smiled.

"Good Boy, that's right. Yeah... take it now, make me proud of you!" he pulled back, once more removing himself from me totally. I adjusted, reached down to pull my cheeks apart as he lined up on my desperate asshole. Then he slammed into me yet again, from cockhead to balls in a massive pounding stroke. Our eyes locked together, we yelled in simultaneous elation, proud of our coupling.

"*YEAH! YEAH SIR* [BOY] *YEAH!*"

I bucked against him, forcing myself up, forcing my pelvis up and onto his penis. My hole spread itself wide, inviting him, pulling him deeper and further into my depths. I smiled, swooned and worshipped as he fucked me, reaming me and taking me to new heights of sexual ecstasy.

"SIR! Oh god Sir, fuck me... fuck me Daddy, fuck me. Yes Sir, FUCK ME!" Dean grinned and complied, resuming his slamming violent assault on my rectum. My body sang in our hot and unrestrained sodomy.

"FUCK ME!"

He began an obscene torrent of commentary. "That's it Boy, open that fucking Hole for me, spread it Boy! Yeah, fucker, take it. You love it don't you, fuck boy? You can't live without this cock in you, my hot SPERM, my fucking LOAD in you. My piss and spooge, my fuckin' CUM is what you need isn't it, huh?"

I nodded wildly, grinning.

"*Tell me*, fuck boy! Tell me what it is you want, what you NEED! Tell me! SAY IT!"

I joined in his litany of sexual violence. "I need it Sir! I need your FUCKING, I need your piss and CUM and your hot sweaty COCK in my asshole! Fuck my ASSHOLE Daddy, fuck me! I gotta have it man! I mean, *SIR*! I gotta have your cock, your PISS oh god Sir, thank you for your PISS and your COCK Daddy fuck me. Fuck me!"

He redoubled his pounding, pummeling me deep and hot, hard and wild. He stretched my rectum to take it, to welcome and accept him as his huge oozing manhood rammed against the walls of my guts. He bashed the back of my prostate, sending hot shooting sensations of manly pleasure and pain coursing up my spine. I lifted my pelvis again and kept up the barrage with him.

"I gotta have it I need it I love it your cock your CUM your PISS Daddy, your COCK oh fuck man fuck me SIR I love it your COCK your COCK your COCK your fucking COCK, oh Sir! Fuck me Daddy!"

"*FUCK* me *FUCK* me *FUCK ME FUCK ME FUCK ME, SIR!*"

He grinned in insatiable horny pleasure, loving the diatribe of need, of homosexual desire, of a hot horny Boy crying for his man's COCK buried within him. He loved it, and in his wild, almost violent way, I knew in that moment he was loving me the only way he could. He reached the edge of sanity as he approached his orgasm and we joined in a repeating chorus of one word.

Together we chanted: it was a mantra, a desire and a need, a want and its fulfillment in one hot, wild action. Two men coupled in that unique, immortal union, his cock in my asshole, his body pouring into me, my body and soul receiving him as we spoke. Each word was punctuated with a smack of his hips as his cock was slammed, buried in me to the hilt again and again.

"*Fuck! Fuck! Fuck! Fuck! Fuck! Fuck! Fuck! Fuck! Fuck! Fuck! Fuck!*" Quicker and quicker the pace, the tempo, as we bucked and reared and fucked.

"Fuck! Fuck! Fuck! Fuck! Fuck! Fuck! Fuck! Fuck!." We reached a crescendo and he began to yell, literally to HOWL as he went over the edge.

"AARGGGGGGGGGGGGGGH! Yeah that's it Boy take it take it here it is my cum for you my seed here's my sperm Boy my spooge, take it yeah that's it I'm gonna CUM! Yeah Boy I'm CUMMING!"

"ARRRGHHHHHHHH!" I slammed myself up, grabbing his butt and ramming him into me, ramming myself onto his fat hard cock as his cum shot, pumped and blasted up into my belly. I felt it spasm, I felt the hot thick goo blast into my tunnel, up against the second ring of my colon, and push into my guts. I took him and cried, screamed with him. We held tight, locked in a hot climax.

"Daddy yes Daddy give it to me, yes Sir, DADDY GIVE ME YOUR CUM! Oh fuck me Daddy! YES!"

He bucked and pounded and the sweat rolled down his face. I spread myself as wide as I could, my hips screaming in pain as I thought the weight of his body and my own forces might well pop them from the sockets. Even that would not have stopped me, and I received his cum as a gift of heaven, as manna from Heaven itself. He filled me, fulfilled me and completed me as I too went into the abyss. I yelled, deeply and fully as my balls split and my cum shot hot and high, up between us and onto us both. A gob splattered the cheap headboard behind me as spurt after spurt of hot manjuice shot up and over us both.

Dean's cum was burrowed, buried in me as mine shot out across my belly, onto him and marked us both. He grinned, pulling me up, up, upward as his cock impaled me. I flopped in helpless spasms of orgasm as my body completed Dean's fucking. He began to sink, to collapse atop me as my racking spasms finally abated. Still I gripped his ass tightly, not wanting to let him pull his invading member from within me.

The sweat stuck to us, my cum gluing us together. For long moments we simply lay in that heap of joined flesh, unable to part, unwilling to break the bond. His beautiful cock began to deflate, to droop and shrink within my asshole as mine lay upon my abdomen oozing the last droplets of seed. At last I was able to look clearly, and see him smiling atop me, pleased, completed as was I.

He slowly pulled back, away. His fine penis finally broke away from my used, abused hole. I let my legs sag, drop back down. I rose and admired him, sweaty and fine, his hairy body strong and proud, his jockstrap highlighting his organs. The side was wet, darkened and stained with sweat and lube, cum... it was beautiful beyond words. His jockstrap, his cock... *Him*. I smiled and sat up, and he stood with his feet apart, daring me.

I leaned forward and slowly took his slick, slimy cock into my mouth to clean him off. I sucked him in and that distinctive, fishy taste of man-sperm mixed with assjuice flooded my senses. I slurped and cleaned him, then he pushed me back onto the bed, my legs apart again.

Without a word, he pushed my legs back, apart, and quickly kneeling between my legs his moustachioed face clamped onto my asshole. Dean gripped my ass-cheeks, tugging them open. His tongue probed into me and I relaxed, then...

He sucked.

He slurped and sucked on me *hard*, pushing on my belly. I relaxed and felt the powerful sensation of him drawing his cum back, away and out of me. It was a birth, an obscene homosexual birth, and he took his offspring back from me in hot felching. He sucked it out, and rose to my face.

Unspoken union joined us and I knew what he would do. My hands stroked up the sides of his body and pulled him onto me, my mouth aching for this perverted, filthy kiss. He spurted the scum into my mouth, and as with our piss, we shotgunned it back and forth, back and forth. Sperm dribbled down my chin, onto his 'stache, and we soared in the obscene, ecstatic joy, the sheer elation of it. I slurped, spewed it back, and he spat, shoved the rest of it into me. He pulled back and up, and looked.

I swallowed and licked my lips.

"You hot FUCKER!" he swore. "You fucking little pig-boy! _Fuck-boy_! Man! Yeah!" He smeared his body on me, swabbed up my cum with his fingers and we did it again, licking sperm and kissing, slobbering and grinding together. I ached in the joyous pain of being worked over, my guts boiling. He lay atop me, stretching on me jockstrap to jockstrap.

"Your turn isn't it?" he said. "Don't even think about the sheets, boy. Do it." I wrapped my arms around his middle, held him close on me...

And pissed.

We floated as nearly a quart of hot piss flowed between us, wet and joined us. I pissed and his cock again thickened in that jockstrap. On and on it went, and I could hear the dripping, splashing as it flowed down my hip and into the sheets. I didn't care. The stream slacked, slowed and stanched. I finished, and Dean smiled again, then pulled himself up from me.

"You hot pig-Boy! You're fine!" I grinned, basking hot in his praise. He quickly moved back to the bathroom and was stripped and running the water hot by the time I got in there. I joined him, and silently, worshipfully washed and cleaned him. We bathed, kissed and rubbed; he received my ministrations as his due, his right. I gave as the finest gift I could. It clicked.

But far too quickly we were done. Dean smacked my ass one more time, and stepped out, grabbing a towel. Again, by the time I could follow he was all but done. He dried, pulled his clothes on and was ready to leave in a flash. He moved back into the room, to the door. I stood naked and wet, sated but saddened to see him leave.

"Yeah Boy, that was FINE. Best I've had, and that's saying a LOT. You were the *Best*." I grinned in pride, and kissed him once more.

He flung his wet, pissed-up greasy jockstrap at my feet and said, "For you." I looked at it in awe. I'd never have dared ask...

"For when you have to have some of Daddy Dean. Don't ever wash it." I picked it up lovingly.

"Oh god _NO_, Sir! I won't! _Ever_!" He smiled.

"I know you won't. Good boy! OK then, till next time..." and with a twist of his wrist, the door opened and he was gone.

It was barely 4:30, but I was done for the weekend. Hell, for the week. I closed the drapes and went to the dry bed, ripped down the covers and sank in, wrapping myself in the scratchy, cheap linens. But the blanket was thick and warm, and within seconds I was asleep. I didn't waken until almost noon on Monday.

Tim did not call, nor was I all that miffed by it. I had a quick lunch on Monday and headed up to see one Michael McClellan at the John Hancock building about a job after graduation. His consulting firm was a good place to get into Chicago business circles, and an assistantship there would also pay well. But he was harried, busy and irritable, and I didn't come off all that well. I figured I had little chance and walked back up toward the Dick-strict. I turned onto Oak Street and realized how close I was to Lila's and to the LoadingZone. I pondered, then headed to Lila's.

I hoped I might see Nick, but it was too early; he'd not be in. I rang the buzzer and the door clicked, I went up. Lila was immaculately dressed as always, and for once had nobody else in the place. She offered me coffee and we sat to talk.

"I haven't seen Tim since I was here with you guys," I started. She smiled, and waited. "I'm not sure if he knows I have to get back to Minneapolis, I'm still in school you know. I'm not going to blow graduation." She agreed.

"Oh heaven's no! But I don't think you'll be seeing much of Tim though, not for a few weeks. He's busy... ahem... 'uptown.' He's got an engagement." I chuckled.

"Conrad?"

"Oh god no! Oh, you didn't hear about it then did you? Oh those two went out after you left, I guess there was *quite* the blow up later! *A-hahaha!* I don't know who expected what, but they couldn't give it to each other I guess!" I had to laugh at that... 'keys right' both of them, and in a big way. Typical. Sure, Tim had fallen for the 'image' crap, but I was damn surprised Conrad hadn't known better. I mean, wasn't he supposed to be some big-deal fashion model in New York as well as here? What a dipshit; both of them.

I thanked her for the talk and the break, and asked her to let Tim know I'd be around after the school term was up. I had several important projects to finish, and the rest of the spring to get through. Then, hopefully, I'd be able to spend some time just taking it easy for the summer. Here in Chi or home in Minneapolis, it wouldn't matter. But I'd have to try to get back down here a couple times, just to see Dean. That I knew.

We finished up and once more Lila offered me some cash to get myself back home. It was kind of her, and I accepted graciously. When I left her place, I gazed at the door of Nick's apartment for a long moment. I hoped I'd see him again too; he still had my clothes and jacket, but I knew they weren't important to me at all. He'd changed my life though, just as surely as Dean had. I wanted to tell him, to thank him, to see him once more. But it was not to be.

Dean. I went back down to the street and hustled back to the hotel. Janice was at the desk, Rex snarled and barked. She didn't look away from her shitty magazine and I went up to my rooms. The place looked so seedy in daylight, so lonely. Without thinking, I picked up the phone and called Dean.

It rang 5 times... then 6. Nothing. I felt something sag within me, and just sat in the nasty hotel chair a good 10 minutes. I tugged at my slacks, then pulled them off. I slowly stripped and then stood naked in the room, stroking my cock and thinking of that hot man... I reached into the drawer and took out the blue jockstrap, crusty and dry, scratchy from our emissions. I sniffed it, licked and sucked on it, chewed and softened it up. Gently, almost lovingly I slipped it over my ankles and drew it on.

I was already rock hard by the time I tucked my genitalia into the pouch, and adjusted the back straps. My bulge was nice, but the body needed more. I was not as hairy as Dean, nor nearly as built. I'd have to work on that; the hair would thicken up in time I was sure. For long moments I simply stroked and admired it, admired myself in it. Wanting and needing, hoping... I was thinking of dialing his home once more when my phone rang. The shockingly loud bell startled me back into the moment, and I answered.

"Hello?"

"BOY? What are you doing?"

"Ohmigod, SIR! I... oh god... I... I'm just standing here and... Oh Sir! I just tried to call _you_!"

"Standing there and what, Boy?"

I caught my breath, quit the stammering and spoke clearly. "I'm standing here in your jockstrap Sir, thinking of you and stroking myself. Realizing how fuckin' thirsty I am Sir, that's what I'm doing."

"Good boy. Good. I just needed to check on you, that's all. I'm busy for the moment, but I'll call you later. Don't do <u>anything</u> till you hear from me, that understood?" I knew what he meant, but it would be goddam difficult not to relieve my hard cock while waiting for him some indefinite time.

"Yes Sir, I'll wait for you. OK."

"Good boy." Click. He was gone.

I ached all the more as the line went dead. Damn. This was not good, I was so smitten with this man and his hot cock, his fine body, his _Piss_. I went to the bathroom and looked at myself in the mirror. Turning on the shower, I let the room fill with steam, thinking about letting myself piss through the jock and maybe catching it in a cup, as Dean had done to feed it to me. I'd drink my own, since I couldn't have his.

I barely had time to think of it and move to get a paper cup when a hot hard pounding was on the door. I knew in an instant it was Dean Cordell. My body jumped, my cock and asshole throbbed and I went to answer it. My hand was on the knob when I remembered him standing there with his penis thrust forward to me last time I'd opened to him. I got on my knees.

With a click, I flipped the latch free and let him open the door himself. He pushed it slowly, and smiled broadly when he entered, seeing me on my knees, in his fine jock, my cock throbbingly hard just waiting for him. And yes, his jeans were open, his hot cock standing straight out, inviting me to service. I opened my mouth and my eyes fell closed as he stepped into the room and quickly shoved himself into my throat to his balls. They mashed on my chin, his cockhead mashed into my glottis, and I gulped, pulled him in and down my gullet and began fellating him even before the door was closed.

He stroked my head and spoke softly. "Yeah that's it boy, take it down. Daddy can't stay and work you over properly, but you get some dick, you can have his piss. That's it suck me boy, take it all now..." and I slurped and sucked as slowly and finely as I was able.

He pulled back, out, and I rose. Quickly pushing me into the center of the room, he offered me a brand new bottle of poppers, larger than I'd seen before. A flat, thick bottle, the same brown as the small ones, he'd already stripped the plastic wrapper from it and motioned me back to the floor. Kneeling before him, I watched as he undid his 501's a bit farther, and let me worship his fine black jockstrap, bulging with his gonads. His slick wet cock hung out the side, hard and wonderful. A tiny pearlescent droplet formed in the slit as I cracked the bottle and took a heavy hit of the powerful liquid.

Three hot hits and Dean moved his hips, flopping his fat dick before me. I opened my mouth and took the tip, just to his scar, and he closed his eyes as I sailed in the rush. He pulsated, relaxed, then...

His *Piss* flowed hot and thick, golden and sweet into my mouth. I sucked harder, letting it fill me, then gulped. He let it flow slowly, deliberately, then opened up full force. I tried to keep up, gulping and guzzling, and reached up to cup his balls. Wanting to put my hands up and squeeze his cock, I ran them up his thighs and without hesitation he grabbed them, holding them tightly, and pulling me onto his manly effusion even harder. I gagged.

He held me anyway, forcing more and more piss into me, up my nose, down my throat. It shot out around his cock, running in rivulets down my chest. Wetting him, wetting his balls and jock. He pissed and pissed, shoving it like a mass, *fucking* it into me. It was not liquid, it was a *Thing*, a living *Thing* coming from him. His Piss. Oh god, PISS! I gagged and the room started to spin. Spots floated before my eyes.

Piss ran down my body, and Piss choked the air from my lungs. Piss filled my face and Piss burned my nostrils. Piss filled my sinuses and Piss was my whole universe. He pissed and I loved it, even knowing I would die in Piss if he did not relent and relent soon. But he did not, would not relent; he pissed. And I drank. Or, tried to drink as best I could. The rush hit me a second time, the room seemed to spin and the world went black.

With spots dancing before my eyes, I found myself being pulled up from the floor, coughing and gagging piss. I could feel the scrapes of new carpet burns being rubbed atop those from the weekend. I was dragged to the bed and Dean flung me face down, his powerful hands set my legs apart and I felt his cock head at my back door. Maybe he lubed himself, I'm not sure, but with none on me he simply slammed himself into me with all the force he had. I was totally conscious in an instant, and screamed outright.

He pressed his hand on the back of my neck, between my shoulder blades and simply took me, assaulting my ass with vengeance and might. I wailed, but I did not protest. I went into the litany of fucking that we'd done the yester-day, screaming at the top of my lungs:

"YES SIR! FUCK ME DADDY FUCK ME SIR! Oh god that's IT Daddy! FUCK ME SIR, fuck your boy in the ASS, fuck my asshole and HURT ME SIR! FUCK ME!"

His cock slammed onto the back of my prostate, pounding into my rectum and beyond, into my colon in wild jolts of electric man-fucking. His assault sent currents of masculine energy coursing through me. I'd never felt so alive, so manly, so fucking hot and FINE as while he fucked me, fucked me into sublime oblivion. Fucked me into himself...

"Fuck me Sir, fuck my ASSHOLE! FUCK ME Daddy and make it HURT! Yes SIR! FUCK ME!"

He groaned and bucked and pounded me harder and joined in the tirade.

"Yeah fuck-boy you like that shit, don't you? You like that hot Daddy-cock up that hole don't you fuck-boy? Yeah that's it! YEAH Boy take it! Yeah hot fuck-boy that's it spread that ASS for me, spread that ASSHOLE open up boy open that ASSHOLE for me! Show me what a fuck-boy is FOR, take this COCK in there and let me fuck you man, let Daddy FUCK YOU, yeah I'm gonna do it boy. YEAH THAT'S IT BOY OPEN UP! Open yourself boy that's it take it I'm gonna CUM YEAH BOY I'M GONNA CUMM FOR YOU! AGGGGGGGH!"

"YES DADDY YES YES YES FUCK ME DADDY! FUCK ME HARD HURT ME SIR! Hurt me with your COCK your COCK I love your COCK Daddy, give it to me give me your CUM!" We bellowed and carried on like banshees as he pounded, slammed himself to the balls again and again, mashing himself against my ass and legs, ramming and tearing into me. It hurt incredibly, beyond 'pain,' beyond words. It was excruciating, exhilarating, liberating. I pulled my ass cheeks apart with my hands and welcomed him, welcomed and pleaded in shouted words of ecstasy for his CUM, his seed, his spunk, his sperm, his load... his manhood. His Essence.

He poured his *Self* into me in hot violent spasms of molten man-iron. Again and again his cock spurted, flexed and jolted, shooting gob after incredible gob of his spunk up my ass. He fucked, rammed and fucked me without stopping until the contractions in his hot prostate subsided. Then with a rough heavy jerk, he yanked his dick from me, leaving me gaping and empty, a void.

With as quick a rough move, his mouth was on my asshole and he sucked, chewed me, *chewed* my asshole, and sucked the cum back. He reached up and fairly punched me in the belly, low, forcing me to give his load back to him, opening my abused, ripped-up hole for his tonguing. I let it go, he sucked it from me. Flipping me over in a flash, he was atop me, and spewed that creamy load into my mouth.

Snot ran down my face from the gagging of my piss-service, and I slurped it down with that mouthful of cum. His eyes gleamed red, forceful and daemonic, a man possessed, a fuck-machine whose essence was the anal conquest of the needy, the willing, the _Worthy_. I sucked it from him, knowing the high rank, the sheer power and position his mighty abuse denoted of me. I loved him for it, he made me a Man in that moment and I loved him from the depths of my soul. I slurped his sperm from his mouth, from my own _asshole_, and ate it. It was not liquid, not something you drink...

But a _Being_, an essence unto itself. Daddy's SPERM. I worshipped him in it, and ate it. I _communed_ him.

He spat the last of it to me with power, and once more raised himself up. His cock was still rock hard, slick and precious with semen and assjuices. I was still gagging a bit and trying to clear the last of his piss from my nasal cavity as he grabbed me by my hair and yanked me to his manhood.

"Clean it up Boy, clean me UP!" he shouted, and willingly, lovingly I took him roughly into my mouth once more. I sucked, sucked hard, and slurped him off, grabbing his ass forcefully, pulling him into me. He grunted and ground himself into me again, letting me finish the work. At last he was content, and yanked back from me.

"Goddam you hot fuck! Hot little fuck-boy! You know how to take care of Daddy, don't you?" I nodded, smiling and wheezing. "Good, good boy." He finally was catching his breath, coming back to this reality, the daemon leaving him.

"Next time Boy, next time... I'm going to get _rough_. I'm going to _hurt_ you Boy, hurt you with my COCK. And you're going to LIKE IT Boy, do you understand?"

"YES SIR! Yes Sir, I do! I DO! I'll be ready SIR!" I ran my hand up his body, fondled his black jock. I dared... I had earned it.

"Sir?" He looked into my yes.

"Please?"

He kicked out of his boots and jeans and slipped the jockstrap off. Just as quickly he was dressed again, yanking his jeans and buttoning up in a flash.

"Good boy." He spat a gob of mucous into his hand and offered it to me. I ate that too, with gratitude.

"Till then Boy... until THEN." He snapped the jockstrap against my chest, and with a spin and a slam he was out the door and gone.

I slowly slipped onto the floor between the beds. I rolled onto my back and reached down, my fingers probing into my own asshole. Two, three... four of them at once. I twisted and turned them, shoved and yanked, rubbing the back of my gland with pitiless force, a paltry imitation of Dean, of Sir, of his COCK. Writhing on the floor with my legs up and apart, I masturbated in anger, in violence and need. I snorted heavily from the insane poppers once again and in the rush, stroked myself to a violent, incredible orgasm. I shrieked as my semen shot up, out and away, sailing easily 4 feet up and behind me. It spattered the bed, the wall, all over me.

I gasped and screamed again, my asshole a burning void of anguish and manly need, of fulfillment and masculine accomplishment. I was wracked with pain and joy, with pride and glowing beauty. Wrenching my fingers inside my tube, I drew out the last smears of Dean's cum and my own rectal mucous, the proof of our fucking. I licked my hand as my body sank down from the power of the climax. I stroked gobs of cum from my chest and face, and ate them too. I smeared more onto the blue strap wrapped about me, about my loins.

I didn't even think about hesitating as my bladder pressed and my urethra opened, and, laying on the floor in Dean's blue jockstrap, clutching and sucking the black one, I pissed and pissed myself.

I swooned and lay there a long, long time. At last, my head was clear enough for me to lift myself up from the beautiful, vile mess on the floor of my room and haul myself into one of the beds. I lay in semi-consciousness thinking, "*Next time* he's going to HURT ME? Oh god, no... no..." Fear washed over me at the idea, but I also embraced how badly I wanted it, wanted and needed him to do just that.

I had to go back to school. The Chicago Nightmare trip was over. I drifted to sleep in the finest agony of after-sex endurance and pain of my life.

FINAL SEMESTER

Back in Minneapolis it was still cold and dreary. The last of the snow was finally dying away and getting to and from class was a lot easier. My apartment was several blocks from the university library, convenient to everything I needed. I'd missed 3 days' classes, but it wasn't a big issue. Inorganic Chemistry was the only one I was at all behind in, but my lab partner quickly brought me up to speed.

Mike was short, maybe 5'5, but muscled, perfectly proportionate. He was a serious crater-face, his swarthy skin pocked and scarred from terrible acne. But on him it actually looked kind of hot; masculine and fine. He was 28 years old he'd told me, 10 years more than me. In his junior year, he was a consummate pragmatist, having done 2 tours, 4 years, in the jungles of Vietnam and Cambodia with the USMC. His beard was thick, almost black, heavy and beautiful. At the start of the term we'd been told to team up for lab, and he'd grabbed me without hesitation. He expected me to carry him, he'd made no bones about it, but he did his share of the work too.

"Yeah I saw the boy-wonder in here and said, *Yup, let's go*. You and me." I wanted to smell him, sniff his crotch and suck his cock but had never had the guts to let him know. Even in the lab his scent was heavy, thick and pungent. I knew he was never 'dirty,' obviously he cleaned often, being addicted to weight lifting and all. But his scent was distracting enough to make working with him difficult.

He showed me his lab abstract and we made plans to get up to the chem lab and finish our work; it was worth 1/3 of our final grade. I got the rest of my assignments organized and went to the sciences building late after lunch. I wanted to go home and nap, feeling dreary and groggy, but it was the only chance we'd have to get our data. Up on the 4th floor, I waited outside lab and Mike was with me right on time. We got our equipment set up and he asked me to explain the concepts to him; he had detailed lecture notes even if he wasn't sure of their importance. I quickly ran it all down and he set the samples as I told him.

It was gas chromatography, using a platinum alloy and various nasty solvents. There was a section of the work that required leaving it to steep itself for a time, and we went out to the parking lot to smoke in his car. He had some smoke. I didn't want to get stoned, but I wasn't going to pass up a chance to be alone with him.

He hit the pipe and passed it to me. I puffed weakly, taking the tiniest puff. It was enough, but quite pleasant. I remembered I still had all that crap I'd swiped and been given in Chicago. "I got a good finger of Thai stick, buddy," I said. "I sure as hell don't want it. Can you use it?"

He grunted, huffing smoke out his nose. "Fuck yeah man, you gonna give it to me?"

"Sure Mike. Why not?"

"You want anything for it? I can't pay much..." he said.

"I don't need the cash man, being *with* you is enough. You enjoy it." He wasn't convinced.

"You sure?"

I paused, just buzzed enough, it was just close enough to the end of the term that I didn't care. "Well, there's something I'd like from you. But it's not payment..."

"Name it."

"I'd like... um Mike, I wanna..." He looked at me; he knew.

"I wanna suck your dick man."

"MAN! What?"

"Yeah, I ain't ashamed. Most guys know I'm a homo."

He smiled. "Yeah I'm kidding you. Why didn't you say so a long time ago buddy? I had a fuck-buddy in 'Nam, I know you like dick." He was shifting in the driver's seat of his Cutlass. "I ain't gonna suck you, and I ain't gonna kiss you. But you can do whatever you like with my cock man, long as it feels good." A wave of relief swept over me, and I moved into position to suck him off in the car.

His body was hairy as an ape's, and he pulled his jeans down almost to his ankles. He didn't care if anyone saw us in there or not, totally confident and sure of himself. He leaned back, pulling his shirt up, and I fondled his chest, his pubes, his balls. The scent from his crotch was more intoxicating then the hash. I sucked him in rapt pleasure, we both loved every second of it.

Mike's cock wasn't huge, but stood hot, harder than iron, and oozed the whole time I slurped and worked him. Precum flavored his shaft, and even that had heavy, thick manly scent. The man's glands produced more pheromones than a wolf; and, like a dominant wolf, he let whomever was nearest and most ready take his cock and his seed. He placed his hand on the back of my head, holding me securely, and fucked deep into my mouth. He bucked and ground me onto him, and in 3 minutes was ready to shoot.

"Fuck yeah, Matt, you're good buddy!" he said. "Here ya go man, take it all; I'm gonna cum!" With a sedate and beautiful pulse, he shot cum up into my welcoming mouth. Three huge spurts of the thickest, hottest and spunkiest cum I've ever enjoyed coursed across my tongue. I took it all and held it. His cock drooled a bit more, I sucked it from the slit.

He pulled back, away from me and pulled me up. "You holding all that?" I nodded.

"HOT! Good deal, let me watch you swallow it! Eat it man!"

I slowly, dramatically gulped, then opened my mouth. I leaned down and slurped his penis again, making sure I didn't miss any. I licked around the tip, down his hard, veiny shaft, and across the upper edge of his hairy, furred scrotum. He let me enjoy it; I knew he was done and the extra treatment did nothing special for him. He enjoyed that I enjoyed his dick, that's all. Mike smiled as I slurped his sperm down and licked my lips.

He was probably the most well-adjusted straight man I've ever met. Totally possessed of himself, he knew it didn't mean squat about _his_ sexuality to allow a buddy to enjoy his penis. And he loved getting his rocks off, shooting a load in the middle of the day. Quite a convenient match for us really. He was right: I should've let him know I wanted it long before. This moment and what I'd learned in Chicago, I resolved I'd never again let such a desire go unspoken. The worst that could happen was I'd be refused. I could defend myself, and those who were truly dangerous weren't attractive to me anyway. Well, mostly... Dean was still difficult to quantify.

The blowjob accomplished, it was time to get back to work. We headed back up to the lab and finished our calculations, using a state-of-the-art chromatography machine to prove our results. It was done. Mike thanked me, and gave me a quick hug.

"I'm done man, won't be seeing you again."

I was dumbfounded. "Why the hell NOT?"

"I already got the exam done, and I got full credit for attendance. I asked Dr. Potter to let me off. He's a vet too, and I'm done. I got an <u>A</u> thanks to you."

"Aw man! Mike..."

He smiled. "Yeah buddy, you shoulda said something sooner. I'd have given you dick all semester. But I'm going to see my kid in Los Angeles. I won't be back till August and you're graduating." He wasn't smug about it, but he was right. It was my fault I'd missed out. He gave me a smack on my shoulder and that was that.

Then I remembered the dope. "You want to come by and pick it up?" I hinted.

He laughed. "OK! OK man, I'll come over! Tomorrow night?"

I agreed and gave him my address. "Save it up for me man!" He grinned and we parted company.

———————————

Mike's arrangement with the chemistry prof got me thinking. There were 4 of my 6 classes I could do that with, even at this point, barely past mid-terms. I'd written my essays for German, played my graduate recital in piano, done the whole set of assignments in math... and like Mike, my requirements for Inorganic would be complete if I wrote the exam. I had to attend orchestra and didn't want to miss it anyway; and needed the information of lectures in Mediaeval Culture to finish my project. I had to attend once a week, that was all. I could spend my time in the pool and let the rest slide.

I went to talk to Dr. Potter and he hesitated, but agreed. "You and Mike both?" he said, "That's a shame. You guys were such a nice addition to the class..." I realized he'd been watching us, my attraction to Mike was obvious. Potter had assumed Mike was dicking me all along I guess.

Too bad it hadn't been so.

But I got back to my apartment and called my buddy Kent, who like me was on the intramural swimming team. He was tall, a lanky Swede, fair and fine. He spoke Swedish, having grown up on an ancestral farm near Brainerd. I'd been raised on our family farm outside Crookston, and we spoke Norwegian, albeit poorly. Kent and I made fun of each other, ridiculing each other's (and our own) heritage, as Scandinavians so often do with one another.

Kent thought my idea a great one, and we made plans to meet at the pool house the next morning. I sucked him off regularly, he was gay but neither of us was interested in anything more. We'd 69 and mutually jack off, suck each others' cocks and even kiss, but we'd never fucked. Without the class schedule, I could service him much more often. And I had other ideas for him now, the horizons Dean had opened for me would please Kent greatly.

The poolhouse opened at 8, but a few team members with special arrangements had keys. We planned to meet at 5:30, and in the cold dark of the morning, we let ourselves in and went to the locker room. We locked the doors behind us; should anyone else come in, we'd hear them. We got into our snug, beautiful Speedos and I stroked Kent's body, feeling him up. He pushed my hand away.

"AFTER you show me a full medley!" he said, and we went quickly into the office to turn on the pool lights. We liked to leave the overheads off, lighting only the underwater lamps. It was eerie, glowing and seductive. Usually we were quite dedicated about swimming our laps, working our bodies, but some days, such as this one, the intention was only to be together, to play and get physical.

We headed into the pool and began splashing about. I swam a few laps, and came up to nip and nuzzle Kent's genitals underwater. He pretended to ward me off, but his cock was swelling noticeably; a most appealing sight. My thermos of coffee was on the side of the deck, and we enjoyed a few cups between laps and playing. After 45 minutes or so, we were ready to call it quits. We still had over an hour to use the place before the phys. ed. classes assembled in the facility. We headed into the locker room and turned on the showers. Kent got under a spigot and I took the one next to him.

He closed his eyes and enjoyed the heat and steam. I was soon on my knees before him and pulled his Speedo down, taking his dick into my mouth. And as many times before, the coffee had him needing to piss as his dick thickened. He motioned me to leave him be, intending to step to the stall and relieve himself. I held him firmly, and did not release his dick from my mouth.

He began to laugh a bit, nervously, and said, "Whoa man, let me go! I gotta get to the can there!" I held him fast, and sucked, holding him tight and hot in my mouth. I stroked his thigh, up to his balls and cupped them gently, and slid my mouth up and down his shaft. Pulling back to the end, I held his corona between my lips as he realized what I was suggesting. His cock jumped and he spoke softly, a secret even alone between us.

"Man, you're gonna take it? Oh man..." He gently thrust his hips forward and I sucked, then we froze, still and quiet, and he let himself open. His slit flared, his body whelmed in hot sensations, and he began to flow.

Piss, he pissed in my mouth.

Holding my head gently, he watched in rapt attention as his urine flowed, hot and thick, strong morning piss flooding into me. I sucked and gulped, swallowing and loving it. My eyes watered and the strength, taste and power of it sent me. Piss. Kent's piss, it was hot.

"Oh man, fuck! Yeah..." he whispered, "Matt, oh my god, yeah buddy. Take it man, that's HOT!" He pissed and poured himself, letting me savor and enjoy it all. His golden goodness flowed, poured into me, and I sucked it, heady and intoxicated. I drank him and he spurted, pumped his dick and flexed, giving me the last drips. He was done. I sucked and held him, both of us not wanting the moment to end.

I rose slowly, my mouth coated with the wonderful man-juice. I quickly leaned into him and before he could protest or resist, I'd shoved my tongue into his mouth in a fine piss-kiss. He stiffened, tasted himself and then pushed me away.

"GODDAM man, no! I don't want that!" He was aghast, but the horny perversion of it was still hot. He'd not be experimenting on the other end of the deal. He stuck his mouth beneath the spigot and took a mass of water, rinsing his mouth and spitting onto the floor again and again. He rinsed himself, his body and Speedo as I watched, proud of myself.

He was finally satisfied, but his cock was almost softened. I got back on my knees to suck him again and he began to thrust himself in and out of my face in quick, short rhythmic jabs. He was totally hard almost instantly. In a minute he was ready, and spurted his cum atop the piss I'd consumed. He bucked and groaned, whispering his encouragement. "Yeah Matt, oh god yeah take it. Fuck!"

Finishing in there, we towelled off and made ready to leave. I watched him dress as I pulled on my jockstrap, sweaty and unwashed for over 3 years. Kent pulled on briefs; I couldn't persuade him to wear his jock. He talked low and secretively, asking me how I'd ever had the nerve to try it, to try drinking _Piss_. He'd thought about it, he said; he had wanted to watch someone drink him. Very briefly I told him of Chicago, of Dean and his powerful domination of me, his pissing and fucking.

He mentioned that with another of his fuck buddies he'd thought about pissing up the boy's ass. I told him I'd not had that, but would be more than willing to try. He was non-commital; knowing that fucking would be a whole level of action he wasn't ready to enter with me. But this hot scene in the shower, he definitely wanted more. And we'd have plenty.

That evening, I'd finished dinner when the knock on the door came. Mike was there, harried and a bit agitated. He was ready to get nasty though, and I knelt to suck his dick in my living room. His jeans were around his knees, and I had a good view of his full masculinity. I wished he would get naked, let me experience the whole of it, but I didn't think he was going to do that. He thrust and face-fucked me gently, both of us enjoying his cock.

His agitation got the better of him though and he pulled me up to my feet. "Here man, take off your pants!" he commanded. I did.

He spun me around, his cock pointing up, hard and hot. His precum oozed as before.

"I need to _fuck_ man, a blow job isn't going to be enough, OK?" I agreed readily, and asked him to get naked. He didn't want to, I could tell, but he finally agreed. He wanted to bend me over the side of a chair and simply fuck my ass, but I prevailed on him.

"Man, it's the only chance we're gonna have, come on Mike! Fuck me properly, OK?" He smiled, and took me to bed. I lay on my back, naked and open for him. He got atop me and in a nice hot flash, slid himself into my ass. I watched his face, his working and bucking as he probed and shoved himself up my asshole, up my rectum. He was getting wild, the need to plant, to furrow and plant his seed was something cosmic, insane. I spread wider and he was on the edge, and I bucked myself to take him and rub my cock on his belly. His hot hairy body reeked of manscent, and this time I knew he had not showered since I'd been with him the day before. It sent me into an orgasmic convulsion just as he hit the limit.

He groaned softly, bucking and driving himself into me as far as he could. His rock-hard cock spurted sperm and sweat coated his chest, his pits. He stank and I leaned up to lick him. He grinned wildly and leaned over me, smearing his hairy armpit onto my face and mouth. I licked and slurped as he finished breeding my asshole. He collapsed atop me, smearing us both in my cum

"Fuck yeah buddy, that's fine. Thanks." His hot breath was on me, in my face and on my neck. I wanted to kiss him, but knew he wouldn't allow that. He pulled his dick from my spunky hole and got up. I was at his side in a moment. "I'm going in here," he said, and he headed out the door. I followed.

As he poised at the toilet, I looked longingly at his beautiful cock, and dared to speak.

"Mike, man... I'll take that too if you want..." He was shocked. He thought about it, then turned slightly away, shielding his penis from my view.

"Oh man, no... no. I'm not gonna let you do that... Aw, man! I can't get into *that*..." I dropped it, and mumbled a quick apology. I left him to drain himself and clean up, and I got some clothes on. I knew his 'straight' sensibilities would be more comfortable the quicker we were dressed. I went into the bedroom so he could slip into his things privately. I returned with his gift just as he was about to leave.

"Here man, I promised you this." He looked down, not meeting my gaze. "Thanks."

"No, thank you Mike. I wish you all the best." He looked up and smiled.

"You too man." I let him out the door and he left my home, left my life forever.

For the next few weeks, Kent and I had regular fun; sometimes piss play, sometimes just hot sucking. It fascinated him that I could take him like that, drink his output and enjoy it so. The mental hurdle was one he could not surmount, nor did he really try to comprehend it. He left it for me to enjoy it, and to do it. The term approached the end; Easter break was upon us and after that, one week more to Graduation. My last party season was just beginning.

I went home to Crookston for Easter, the university was all but deserted. I returned before most students. Kent and I had plans to spend a few nights at my place. Twice a day he fed me piss and we sucked one another. I wanted him to fuck me, I wanted to fuck him. But it he ignored my hints and we left things as they were. Spring break was over, and classes would resume for the final push. The big weekend of partying before Graduation was upon us.

A WILD INVITATION

Kent and the men of his fraternity had big plans for that weekend. The spring party and cruising night were coming up quickly and they needed to make plans as to what the special, wild features would be for the party of 1978. Being all 'straight' guys, there was plenty of talk about getting a few sorority girls to come by and get them drunk, get them upstairs and get into their panties and blah blah blah, enough to make you puke. *Every* straight-boys' frat party is supposed to be some kind of orgy; the truth is usually far more prosaic. In any case, saner heads prevailed and they weren't real hep on committing a gang rape that close to graduation. And being horny men in their late teens and early twenties, most all of them at some point or another had had a j/o buddy or even blowjob partner. Plenty of them still had a homo pal on the side to relieve their tensions. A heavy dose of sex in the party-mix would not be unreasonable...

I was not a regular for any of those guys, but I'd sucked a couple of them off from time to time. Having my own apartment since I'd come to the University in Minneapolis at age 18, I wasn't a member of any frat-house, but welcome in several. Hooking up with frat-boys was usually after a game or a meet, after they'd gotten rid of the girlfriend for the night and needed to bust a nut. I even had one of them get naked with me and got his cock up my ass. Too weird for him though; a couple hard pumps and he blew his load, and then he never acknowledged me again. Oh well, he wasn't all that great in the first place.

The guys got talking about what would be the hottest, wildest party yet. I don't know if it was Kent or someone else who first broached the topic, but somehow the idea of a piss party came up. Can you believe it? A straight-boy fraternity, but they wanted to have a scene where everyone is flashing cock and guzzling beer and having piss contests... who could shoot the farthest, who held the most, you name it.

Maybe they could trap a freshman or someone and piss all over him? Put him in a tub and make him wallow in it? Maybe even make him drink it...? Wouldn't that be wild, hold him there and stick your dick in his mouth and make him drink it right from the hose?

But I'll bet dimes to dollars on <u>any</u> day it was Kenton who said, Hmmm sure. I KNOW SOMEONE WHO WILL DO IT! They were aghast. How bizarre! How utterly wild! They were horrified, shocked, they were *fascinated*... But that's the intoxicating, obsessive quality of piss. The more they thought about it, the more they talked about it, the more they all wanted to *DO IT*. To experience it, to see it happen. Kent said it could happen, it really could. They said, OK then, get on it, *make* it happen.

He didn't tell me the nature of those talks for years afterwards, so I'm not sure on the details. I *am* sure he glossed over the more disparaging comments (his own too) made about this homo who drank piss and loved it. But, they decided one afternoon in early April that the Great Piss Party would take place. And as I heard it from him (and others too,) <u>nobody</u> dissented. Whether that was a case of 'groupthink' or real interest I don't know. But the decision to hold this party was, for the Deltas, unanimous.

It was Kent's responsibility to make sure I was on board. That I got their early, and if not willing to accommodate them all, to make sure I got stoned enough that it would happen anyhow. Willing or not.

We were in the shower together after swimming, as we so often had done, and Kent wanted to play. He got me back into our favorite stall and began feeding me his cock. Then he leaned back and I knew he was ready for me to drain him. Woof! I was ready too. But he stopped and looked down at me.

"How much piss do you think you could really hold?" he asked. I shook my head.

"Hell I don't know. When we've been drinking a lot of beer I can hold a good 14-16 cans. That's 6 quarts, a gallon and a half."

"Mmmmm..." Kent mused. "Wow, that would be a HELL of a lot of piss. Ever thought about taking that much?"

"Yeah well, I've wondered how much I could actually hold. When you are totally full, you give me something more than half a quart. That's totally full, where you're hurting to go. Six quarts would be 10 or 12 guys like you, and I bet I could hold more than that. Would be fuckin' wild to try though... hot!"

He paused, let me resume sucking his cock. But quickly he pulled back again, and continued.

"Want to try? Want to see how much you can really take?"

I wondered where he was going to find a dozen men (or more) who wanted to give me piss all at the same time. He hardly ever went to the gay bars, and he sure didn't know any other water-boys. Suddenly I had an inkling where, a damn good idea where from, and the thought intrigued me.

"What the hell are you guys up to?" I asked.

"Well, just that. We're having a beer party, and the guys want to see someone really get into piss. We got a bathtub, a piss trough... there's gonna be 18 men and a couple kegs of beer. Gonna drink until the beer is gone or we all pass out. You up for it? Want to be the pissboy?"

"Jesus Kent... you're not kidding are you? How did you get Bill Barlow and Bill Macey to go along with THIS idea? Those big fag-haters?"

"They're not fag-haters; besides, they like you." I winced at that. I still tried not to let it be *too* obvious, but hell. Everyone knew I was gay. And he was right. The leaders of the Delts did like me. But this would change everything. And I knew it too.

"You guys have actually talked about this?"

"Yup. And I told the Bills you might be into it for the party."

"Wow. Damn."

He pushed his thick dick towards me and let me suck again. He relaxed, the piss began to flow and I sucked it deeply. I pawed up his firm belly, his smooth abdomen. He gave me a good dose, then stopped again.

"So you in?"

I looked up, his cock still in my mouth, then let it flop out as the realization hit me.

"You already *told* them I'm in, didn't you?"

"Well... yes I did."

"Shit Kent! That was pretty fucking brazen of you."

"But I knew you'd do it Matt. You'll love it. Besides, I can't back down now."

Oh no. He couldn't, that was no joke. And it gave me a way to accept without the wrangling I would've had to go through to do such a thing on my own, wrangling about my own sanity for starters. I couldn't let him down. I nodded and craned forward for more of Kent's dick and piss.

He let me take it then, his cock pulsing as he thought about the scene; himself 'straight' as far as all of them knew, but giving me his piss in front of a willing and cheering audience. An audience that would then join him. He thrust forward, then relaxed again. This time he let it flow till I drained him. I burped and smiled, then got up from my knees. I wanted him to fuck me for this one, I wasn't going to get him off in the stall. He'd have to come up to the room and fuck me. He knew it too.

He wrapped an arm around me, then grinned. "Yeah buddy! It'll be the hottest party the Delts have ever had! And you'll be the reason it is!"

I smiled too, still filled with trepidation. I was amazed at how jittery I felt, just thinking about it. But it was more than a fantasy, a hot daydream of manly piss on a cosmic scale. This was going to happen. And I had no idea how those 'straight' men would react in reality; all of them pissing and getting into some homo (me!) sucking them together. But I knew I had to do it. For Kent.

Oh hell, fuck Kent.

I wanted to do it. And I would.

We finished in the locker-room and headed out. After dinner, Kent stopped by my place. I simply opened the door and let him in, and walked to the bedroom. We were naked in no time, and he fucked the HELL out of me. The living hell. After he shot his thick load of cream up my tunnel, he lead me to the shower and rinsed off. The he gave me my favorite dessert. I thought about cock after pouring cockload of piss from his frat brothers as he satisfied me. If I had held any doubts, they were now gone. I couldn't wait.

––––––––––––––

A few days later Kent called me and asked me to come to the Delta house. I knew what it was about, getting the agreement and the details set for their party. When I arrived, Kent and the Bills were in the lounge. Barlow (the president) had told the rest of the guys to make themselves scarce for a couple hours. Nobody else was around. But I figured the others knew something was up and might be lurking around a corner or waiting to see who came out of the house after this meeting. They invited me in and gave me a beer. Bill lit up a cigarette.

He cut right to it. "So Matt... Kent told us you're up for some wildness at our party. You know what we mean?"

"Yup I do Bill. He told me what you guys want. I'm interested."

He huffed smoke and leaned back. "You really think you can handle 18 beer drinking boys all night and drink our piss? ALL our piss? You like sucking dick that much?"

"I like sucking dick anytime Bill. And I like piss. And I'm not afraid to say I've been watching a few of you guys for the last couple years. I'll do it. But..." I paused, Bill waited. Here it was.

"What do you want in return?"

"Protection," I said. "I'm not stupid enough to think this isn't going to get around. Hell, it'll be the talk of the whole school; your parties always are. But I don't want to be cornered after a game and beaten into pulp, or raped by a bunch of fat hooligans from Kappa Tau, that kind of shit." I paused and lit my own smoke.

"I just want you guys to own up to it too. It isn't going to make anyone a queer or make YOU gay because you all got wild one night. But if push comes to shove, I want you to own up that I'm a buddy of the Delts, and that you'll look out for me too. That's all."

Bill looked at Kent, then to the other Bill. They nodded; he nodded. "OK Matt, you got it. We'll say it just happened, nobody's fault and nobody really knows anything. Things got wild like a Delt party does, and you're still welcome anytime. We'll back you up when you need it."

"OK then. You're on. _All_ of you!" They all chuckled at that and relaxed. Kent went to get more beer from the kitchen and Barlow walked to the window. I turned to Bill Macey. His blond hair and moustache glowed, his blue eyes twinkling. "So... this sound like fun?"

He smiled, grinned. "Yeah, it's gonna be a wild close to our college days, that's for damn sure." The others were still out of earshot.

"Want a trial run beforehand? Just you and me?" I whispered.

He twisted in his chair, shocked. His hand went to his crotch in a defensive reflex. "Um, uhhhh... no man, that's OK. That's OK..." I winked.

Kent and Bill B rejoined us, we had another round and talked over the details. Where the piss play would be, the trough, who would supervise. We decided on the concrete floors in the basement, the 'Dungeon' of course. The floor plan was basically a mirror of the first floor, a great room and entrance hallway, some lesser rooms on the sides. I'd be in the great room, scantily clad. A jockstrap or gym shorts, no shirt. I'd be ready to take all comers: in the trough, on my body, down the gullet. _Pisser's Choice_ I called it, and they roared hysterically. We laughed, speculated, fantasized. I thought I saw some bulges starting to appear in the Bill's slacks, but I wasn't sure. Kent's boner was obvious, and he didn't care.

The men would be sent to the Dungeon when it was time to relieve themselves; all would participate. The Bills would make sure no-one declined, so that none of the brothers could say he wasn't part of the action. Either Kent or one of the Bills or Don Camden would be at the door or inside the room at all times to make sure things didn't go _too_ far... I would have all the beer, smoke and whatever else I wanted. I was satisfied with the arrangements.

We had a couple more drinks, talked and laughed, then it was time for me to leave. I excused myself to visit the head before I went back home. It hadn't occurred to me until then that nobody had used the bathroom the whole time I'd been there. Skittish, I figured. I pissed into the bowl of the hallway bathroom, imagining how things would go on Friday night... into Saturday morning... maybe into Sunday. Who knew? It'd be awesome, I knew that much. My stream splashed and echoed; I watched in fascination.

I finished and opened the door. Nobody was in the hall and I went back into the lounge to get my jacket. Macey stood alone beside the coffee table. He glanced at me quickly and looked away. But he made up his mind, and looked at me directly.

"The guys had to go up the hill to the provost; about that guy we booted..." I nodded.

"Yeah OK Bill; I'll be going. Tell Kent I'll talk to him tomorrow."

"Sure. I'll tell him." I put my jacket on and started to leave. "Hey Matt..."

"Yeah Bill?"

"Um, nobody's here right now and I was wondering... did you... Did you really mean that about a trial run?"

I smiled sheepishly; mirroring his own trepidation. I spoke softly. "Yeah Bill, I meant it. You don't want anyone to know though, right?"

He nodded. "No man, we can't let anyone know about it, OK?" The 'we' was good, he wouldn't be saying it was all my fault should something go wrong. He wanted to play, to experiment.

"Well, maybe here isn't the best idea? You'll need to take some time, get comfortable, relax... I can show you."

"Yeah man, that's what I need. What I want. Where... what... where do you think...?"

"That's easy bud; my place. I'll go out, you make some noise like you're going out for errands. I'll meet you at the end of the block and drive you up, then bring you back. I'll make sure nobody sees us."

Mace nodded and smiled. I went out the front door and got in my car. I watched him through the main window. He headed into the kitchen at the back of the house, and the light went out. I waited about 90 seconds, then slid the car into gear and headed to the corner. As I neared, Bill came from behind the neighboring house, having gone up the alley. I slid to a stop and he hopped in. In 5 seconds we were clear of Frat Row and on our way to University Gardens Apartments. Bill kneaded his crotch the whole way.

We pulled into my parking lot and silently got out. Bill walked quickly, I thought he was worried about being seen, then I remembered we'd had 3 beers, or maybe it was 4... he was ready! All the better; a straight guy trying to piss into a man's mouth for the first time often has that 'stage fright,' I'd learned. Pee-shy they call it. This would make it a LOT easier for him. He wanted it, needed it.

We entered the apartment and I tossed my jacket onto the chair. Bill did likewise, his slacks bulging prominently. He looked around, stroking his crotch, then headed towards the hallway, the bathroom. He didn't need directions. I followed him and he had the light on and his pants open by the time I got myself into the room.

"Man! I can't wait any more!" he said, and I dropped to my knees. I grabbed his dick snugly and cupped his balls as his pants slid fully to the floor. I could only barely notice how beautiful he really was, we didn't have time. I took his cock into my mouth slowly, making him hold back a bit, gripping the tube lest he blast me and startle himself. I sucked and slobbered him up, then slid back, just the head of his fine cock in my lips. His bush was blond too, LONG hairs tickling my face as he mashed himself forward and I waited.

I waited and sucked the tip of his cock. Nothing. I looked up and Bill had let his head loll backward, his eyes closed. Instinctively he was trying to relax, just let it happen, yet that stage fright held him back. I waited, holding him in my mouth. But nothing.

He opened his eyes and sighed. "Damn!" He pulled back from me, then stroked himself a bit, admiring his own cock. He smiled, but spoke with a hint of embarrassment.

"I was afraid that might happen. I'm full, damn I gotta go! But I can't."

He paused again. "That nice? You think that's a nice dick?"

"Damn Mace, you know that's a nice dick! Fuck man, you're *Fine!*"

"Aw thanks Matt..." He was genuinely pleased. It once more amazed me how so many men have such a poor image of themselves, and the ones who have a high image of themselves are such assholes. I wanted Bill to be able to perform, to enjoy this, as much as for *himself* as for me. More. Really I did, as much as I wanted to suck the piss out of this hot, hot man.

I relaxed a bit and stroked his belly. My fingers tangled in his beautiful bush and he adjusted his stance. Suddenly he said, "Oh man! Here! HERE IT COMES!"

In a flash I had that wonderful shaft of man-meat back in my lips. Just as quickly he opened up and his piss began to flow. I gulped and swallowed quickly; I was determined that as much as I had ever wanted to take it all, this time I would show Bill what it was about. No gagging, no sputtering, no piss out the nose. That would be fine in the trough; right now I wanted to suck him and let him enjoy it.

I had to hold that hot cock snugly though and control the flow as I usually did; otherwise the spewing and spluttering would be exactly the result. He pissed; I drank. He leaned back a bit, his hips forward and his cock thick, hot and funky as the juice poured out. I stroked his thighs, his belly and butt cheeks as I nursed and drank. He pissed a full hot stream, he was in as much ecstasy as I was.

The light on, he looked down and watched as his fluid poured out his slit into my willing, thirsty gullet. Absentmindedly I thought how cool it was that he could be so secure, the lights on, no pretending he wasn't getting into some hot KINKY sex with another man. He watched, he pissed, I sucked and drank, and we both took what we wanted from the situation.

"Oh Matt, yeah! Yeah man, goddam... take it. Oh buddy, drink it. Fuck..."

I gulped and guzzled, and the pissing continued. I squeezed and released, pressed and relaxed on his dick, letting the flow go hot and hard, then slower so I could catch up. I gulped and nothing spilled around my lips. I didn't lose a drop. I drank him, he pissed.

I released the pressure on his tube and let the last 30 seconds of his load go unabated. He poured out, pushing on his muscles and made the last spurts powerful indeed. I took it; then slid his cock to the back of my throat. Only then did I realize how big he truly was. Thick and hot, tumescent, all but fully hard, he reached easily between my tonsils and probed beyond. Big, hard, thick... damn, he was nice.

Bill Macey ground himself forward a bit and pushed into my gullet, his hands stroking across the top and back of my head, feeding my dick. He slowly fucked my face like an expert, like feeding a man his glorious cock was exactly what he was built for. Indeed, he was, but I didn't know HE knew it!

Mace was drained but he didn't stop. I sucked and his cock got harder. He leaned over me, then pulled back. "Oh man, damn! Wow Matt, goddam!"

I smiled and licked my lips, then he stuck hands into my armpits and pulled me to my feet. He pulled me in close, then kissed me. I about died. Straight guy, huh?! Oh yeah! Damn that was a fine kiss.

He mashed his naked flesh against me, groping down my body, stroking my back, my ass, all the while kissing and holding me. At last we broke the embrace.

"Geez Mace! Damn you're hot!"

"Matt... buddy... I gotta know. I gotta have... come on." He tugged at my arm and we moved out of the bathroom and down the short hallway. Bill reached out and snapped on the light in my bedroom, and wiggled his pants completely off. Then his shirt. He stood in the light, beautiful and naked, and I quickly undressed too. I moved up to him and once more we kissed. He leaned back, and together as if in slow motion we fell onto the bed, me atop his warm body.

Licking and kissing, he ran his hands over me, down my back, up my chest, then into my crotch. He took my cock and moaned lightly as he felt the size and hardness of my own meat. "Yeah man, yeah..." Mace wrapped his legs around me and lifted them, it was obvious what he wanted. What he needed.

I reached to the bedside table and opened the drawer, taking out the poppers and the lube. Bill ground up against me harder, knowing that the bottle of grease meant immanent penetration, complete fulfillment. He wanted it. He lifted his legs, grinding his basket against me as his asshole puckered and clenched when my oozing cockhead touched against it. I looked into his eyes.

"Have you ever done this before?"

"No man, no. It's cherry. C'mon man, take it. Give it to me, let me know what you can do!"

"Man Bill, hell yeah! But you got a nice big dick buddy, real nice dick."

"Aw man yeah, but it's *your* dick I need. Put it in me man, I wanna feel it. Fuck me Matt, c'mon..." He said it again, softy. "*Fuck me.*"

"I will man, I will. I just want you to know, my cock's about like yours. It ain't small buddy... I don't want to hurt you..." I trailed off.

"Matt man... you won't. I know you won't. You know what you're doing, what I want. C'mon man, let's fuck. *Fuck me,* man! Please?"

I flipped the lid off the lube and took a nice dollop, then slid my greasy fingers onto his hole. I lubed him up, only slightly letting my fingertips enter his tight pucker. He writhed a bit, lifted his legs higher, wider, and clenched his eyes. He was trying to relax, waiting. I positioned myself, my rock-hard phallus touching the lightly furred pucker of his asshole. I pushed, slowly, gently. He tightened, then moaned. That hot hole flexed, pulsed and relaxed. Damn he had control! I pushed again and the first inch of my cock slid into him.

A quick short gasp told me he was fully aware, and also fully ready. Again I pushed my hips downward, forward and sank another inch and a half into him. His eyes flickered, then opened, his legs lifted high and wrapped about my shoulders. I slid back a bit, then in farther. Halfway... a full 4" into his rectum. He gasped.

"Oh god Matt... oh god go slow buddy! Oh man, yeah..." He writhed again, and forced himself upward, impaling his own body onto the next 2" of my dick. Three-quarters; one more tug, one more pulse and I'd be in him fully. I reached for the poppers and twisted the cap. I took a quick huff, and relaxed. Once more I pressed downward and into Bill's fine ass.

"What's that?" he asked, and I handed him the bottle.

"*Just inhale it*," I said clearly. "Don't get the liquid on you or up your nose, just the fumes man. It'll make it easier. Get ready man, you're getting *fucked...*"

He looked at the bottle warily; I took it back from him and held it beneath his nostril. I blocked the one while he huffed through the other, then switched sides. He'd noticed how I'd done it so he wasn't bad for a first snort. The rush hit him and I saw his eyes roll back. I pushed in hard, fully, and buried my cock in his ass right up to my balls.

"Oh fuck YEAH MATT! Goddam, yeah man! Fuck me!" He bucked and writhed and I began a slow, steady rhythm shoving my 8-incher into him, pulling back and sliding in to the root again. On we went, fucking slowly, sensuously. I leaned in to take a kiss, then wrapped my arms tightly around him.

I held him in a tight ball, his legs up over my shoulders, his ass spread open, filled with my hot cock. I fucked him slowly, steadily, firmly. Then I picked up the pace and began a deep, hard stroke from cockhead to balls, again and again. He moaned.

"Shit man, yeah! Oh god Matt YEAH! Fuckin' ay buddy, fuck me!" He was really on the edge, almost out of control. He bucked and got louder, "Goddam it man, FUCK ME! YEAH BUDDY! Fuck me, oh man fuck me fuck me fuck me fuck me... oh god... oh god we're *fucking... fucking...*" His eyes closed and he moaned again.

"*Fuck me!*"

I slammed myself into him hard and deep, and held him impaled on the full length and width of my substantial shaft.

"AHHHHH! *FUCK ME!*" he yelled, and I was on the edge too. I pressed him back and down, and shoved my cock into him as hard as I could, holding him tight. My balls boiled and I began to howl and buck on top of him.

"Fuck yeah Mace, yeah buddy! Here I cum man, I'm gonna shoot it! Oh god man I'm CUMMING!"

He ground himself upward and I swear his asshole spread open that much more as my load exploded into his guts. Three, four... five full hot spurts of cum shot up inside him, while he gritted his teeth as if it scalded him from inside out. The sweat stood out on his forehead as I came, unloading my manly seed inside him.

"Fuck Bill! Yeah, I'm cumming buddy! Take it, here it is! I'm CUMMING!"

I strained atop him, every vein in my neck standing out, the cords taut. We were frozen, locked together in a pose of horny sodomy, our faces masks of hot pleasure bordering on pain. Mace lay beneath me, his ass spread out, impaled, pinned to the bed by my cock. It spurted again, dribbling and draining into him. I pulsed, dripped a bit more, shot the last of my sperm. We began to relax, and I dropped on top of Bill with a gasp. He held me, his legs still tight around my shoulders as his cock rubbed and oozed against my belly as he writhed.

"Matt, Matt... oh god Matt, I'm gonna cum too! Oh fuck man, I'm cumming!" I lay there, all but exhausted, yet savored the feeling of his cock pulsing and spurting against me. I held him tight and kissed him as his juices shot between us. The slime of his hot thick load pasted us together, and as his orgasm subsided from *le petit mord* back into this world I kissed him again, slow and deep. We breathed together, fucked out and sated.

Lying tangled in our sweat and spooge, we stayed a long, long moment without a sound but our breath. At last he spoke softly.

"Oh my god Matt. Oh my god... I never knew. Man, that was awesome.

God man, where have you been all these years?"

I looked deeply into his eyes and laughed lightly.

"Been across the lecture hall from you, dreaming about your piss and your asshole, buddy! Been here all along." Bill chuckled too, and stroked me one last time. We parted and began to clean ourselves and each other up, in silence.

He was dressed in no time, and walked into the living room. The tentative steps he took showed me I'd done him right for his cherry-poppin'. He would feel it for quite some time, but I was also sure that was not unwelcome.

"Ready?" I asked, and he nodded. Back in the car, I drove slowly back towards Frat Row, and pulled to the side of the darkened street a block from the Delta house. I shut the car off, and we simply sat a moment, together. There were no words for his feelings; nor for mine either. At last he leaned over to me and spoke softly, almost inaudibly.

"Matt... thank you. I've wondered about this for years. Now I know. Matt, I think I love you."

I was shocked, but not offended.

"Mace, you're overwhelmed right now. Enjoy the body, enjoy the sensations. We can have more if you want," he was already grinning and nodding a firm *Yes!* "But you don't want to make that kind of a choice now. There's too much yet to learn."

He seemed OK with that, but pulled me close one last time, and planted a long, slow kiss deep into my mouth. I held him, savoring his scent and body. At last we broke the kiss and he opened the door. Quietly he slipped from the car and walked toward the frat house and disappeared into the shadows.

THE DELTA HOUSE PARTY

Friday afternoon was warm and clear, unseasonable but most welcome. The guys had prepared the house nicely with a bar, ice tubs for the beer kegs, lounge areas. The smoking room had a rolling table and trays, papers and pipes, lighters... I arrived at 7:30, the scheduled kick-off was to be at 9:00.

The Bills and Kent were already setting up a keg and getting it ready to be tapped. The rule though was they could have canned and bottle beer until the "start," then everyone would be present for tapping the first barrel. They dumped ice around it, the tin washtub it was resting in was cold and frosted, condensation already running down onto the old rug that surrounded it.

I asked Macey to show me the preparations in the basement. He lead me down the stairs and into the great room. It was wild. The concrete floor was bare, but there were several wooden barstools around the walls, a couple here and there, for guys who wanted to sit and watch the action. The lights were covered with red and blue globes, plastic. The result was a rather subdued violet light, very enticing and horny even for an empty room.

In the center a claw-footed iron tub, in surprisingly good condition. The porcelain was clean, the interior of the tub intact, with only minor cracking. On a table to the side were a number of towels and such, as well as plastic beer cups. They'd set it up pretty well. There were some other details that were truly inspired...

I nodded my approval and turned to Mace. "Nice. Who do you think is going to go first?"

He chuckled a bit. "Not sure... but either Bill B or Kent... or me. You got a preference?"

"Nope... who ever has the balls to get the action started, hehehe. Gonna take you all man, but I hope it's you."

He smiled, remembering the scene we'd shared a couple nights before. I figured his asshole was ready for action at some point; probably not until Saturday night though. We'd not get a chance until way later into the party, and by then even we would no doubt be about ready to crash, not fuck. But I'd be prepared if he was, and if we got a chance to slip away and get nasty.

I had myself ready: I'd brought a duffel bag with clothes, some accessories, and was ready to get into the scene with abandon. I planned to smoke some with the guys as things got going, then head to the basement play-room right about when the heavy drinkers, Mike Tollefson and Gordie Smith, filled their cups for the 3rd time. I figured that would be a good indication for timing.

We puttered around, getting things ready as the frat guys got back from classes, from supper, here and there. They were all present by 8:45. Kent and Bill Barlow pulled me aside. The roar of laughter and hepped-up men talking and carrying on echoed from one end of the house to the other. He'd called for head-count in the main room at 9:00 sharp.

"Matt, I didn't know if I should do this or not, but... a few of the guys wanted to invite friends. We got some out of town Deltas and a couple others I allowed..." He tried to gauge my reaction, I was deadpan. "This changes the agreement, I know..."

"Well man, how many are you talking about?"

"Seven more, but Garry Karlsen already went back to Moorhead; so there is a total of twenty-four."

I smiled vaguely. He continued.

"Course, if you're not going to be able to handle all of us, we gotta understand. We're all hoping you'll still go through with it. At least for the first few hours, you know?" Bill Macey came up, looking a bit worried; he'd just heard about the change in plans and knew it was a critical moment. If they didn't make things pretty nice pretty fast, I could well walk out on the deal.

"Well man, that's not such a big difference, but it makes things kinda questionable for me. I've tested myself, to see just what I can really handle, and 18 o'you was going to push me right to the edge to begin with. Even beyond. I didn't want to be puking and all, but 7 more I think is going to guarantee that's just what'll happen." They looked a bit concerned, but I reassured them.

"I'm going to do what I can though, this is going to be too wild to miss."

"Atta boy! Yeah! Cool."

Big woofy stud John Baecker came in from the kitchen. "Hey Bill, Bill, Kent... when we gonna get this shindig going man?"

Barlow swung about, "Hey Johann... you met our party boy here? This is Matt."

Baecker smiled, but would not extend a hand. "Yeah, I know Matt. We had Chem IV together last year." I sure as hell remembered him in the lecture hall; he was hotter'n a $2 pistol and hornier than a 2-dicked donkey. He'd fuck anything, any time, any where, for any reason... girls, boys, men, women, maybe donkeys too. Nobody knew for sure. For the most part, that was true of all the Delta boys. Horny bastards one and all. And for the most part, all wildy hot men too. There wasn't any secret about the fact that uglies did not make pledge. Deltas had to have looks, money, looks, a GPA of 3.0 or better (give or take a whole grade point...,) looks and money. And looks were very important too.

Mace answered for us all. "The doors are going to be locked at NINE, and we crack the first keg once that's done. We're almost ready, so if you wanna get everyone into the main lounge we can formally begin." John thought that was a great idea; of everyone, I think he was most fascinated about a night of drinking, debauchery and watersports. It was a well-known 'secret' that he and Gus Gustavson were fuck-buddies; Johann was _never_ bottom. But Gus could be a hot top too, and had not only a girlfriend but a child. Johann could validly expect to get his rocks off at least once during the night.

Truth be told, ALL the boys expected that; and even if not into man-to-man sex, they would be tonight.

A cry went up in the lounge. At least a dozen wild partiers yelled in unison, _"NINE O'CLOCK!"_ and we all headed into the main room. They gathered around the washtub and beer keg. Everyone had his own beer mug or stein; many from school and family trips to Germany, Norway and Sweden... those were scary. Frosted glass with heavy handles and enameled insignia, and held a liter, some 1.5 liters... woof!

The Bills took the center; I was just to the side. "Hey Delta Men!" Barlow called out. "Welcome to the Spring House Party. We're all here... and we all know the routine. Tonight though, since it's getting hot and we're all ready to party, we got a special guest who's going to serve us all in a very special way!" There was general snickering and rude talk, more than one of the guys was groping himself already. A few were saying 'can't wait to see THIS' and so on.

"But we have to get the rules straight first. Mace, lock the door." Macey went to the front door and using his main key locked the deadbolt from inside. "Nobody else comes in, nobody is going out. We all agreed on this, and everyone will take part; nobody is going to say later he wasn't in on it. Those who didn't want to play have left and we also have a couple alumni in for the weekend. Introduce yourselves to them later. Now count off."

Kent started, and with unrehearsed precision the roll was called, going around the room. There were already 27 present, but I didn't complain. Barlow nodded approval and said, "All accounted for, now we gotta get DRINKING!"

A wild cheer went up and Barlow had to yell to finish his remarks. "HEY! Most importantly we wanna thank Matt for coming. This wild pervert is gonna show us all a whole new deal; welcome our hot PISS BOY!" They cheered and clapped, a couple smacked me on the back and shoulders. I took a mock bow and Bill got to the point.

"But now... since he's going to be the one who drinks this whole keg, whether it's from his mug or recycles yours," (wild horny laughter,) "It's his duty and privilege to tap the barrel!" With that, he handed me the tapper and I moved to the basin.

Straddling the beer keg, I made as if I was fucking it, and yanked the plastic disc off the mounting hole, 'busting her hymen,' as it was called in keg parties. I quickly screwed the tap into it and then... flipped the lever while pointing the nozzle around the room. I sprayed most everyone, myself most of all. I had beer soaking my shirt and T-shirt, but my clothes would be going away soon anyhow.

Then I called out, "Give me your poor, your WRETCHED, your thirsty masses aching for RELIEF! Give me your beer and your BEER PISS, MEN!" Once more the room echoed with cheers and insanity, as the guys filled their mugs and began the night's perversion.

Again a cigarette was being passed; I grabbed it from Johann and claimed it as my own. I went with Mace into the kitchen and began to undress. I gave him my boots and shirts, stripping down to just my jeans and jockstrap. I had intended to wear the leather cock strap I'd gotten in Chicago from a guy named Dave Marquette, but in taking a trip to a porn store, I'd found a steel ring. I had only jacked off with it twice, but I liked it a lot. I had 4 bottles of Rush and a large container of lube as well, 'just in case.'

Bill Macey shoved my gear into a cupboard by the back door and smacked me on the ass. His bone was already prominent, and he slugged rapidly from his liter-mug. I could see the blue and white pattern and the word 'Hofbrauhaus' on the side.

He sidled up to me, close, and whispered in my ear. "I wanna be first man, but I don't know. I don't want to get stage fright or anything you know..." I grunted.

"Maybe we should check out the special arrangements downstairs," I suggested. "Make sure it's all ready and holding up?"

He nodded and we were going to the stairway when Baecker came in. He grinned at me, leering. "So you wanna taste of this dick, faggot?" Barlow was right behind him and bristled a bit; it was too early for antagonism.

"Man, no need for that kind of talk..." I stopped them.

"Hey screw it; Johann knows I'm a faggot, I know I'm a faggot, and yes... I've been wanting to suck that COCK for years. You ready to go, trying to be first or what?"

He laughed, my bluntness had completely disarmed him. "Almost, faggot!"

"Well then, let Mace and me make sure everything's ready and come on down! Give us 2-3 minutes OK?" He growled in agreement and headed back to the lounge, no doubt to find a retinue to cheer him on when he whipped it out and fed me. Egoist...

ROUND ONE

IN THE TROUGH

Macey and I quickly tromped down the stairs and adjusted the lights. Everything was ready. Behind the tub Gustavson and 2 of the guest Delts had built a sort-of platform and wall of plywood. Four steps lead up to the platform which was large enough for 3, maybe 4 men to stand on at once. The wall screened them from the tub side, but...

On the wall they had mounted an honest-to-goodness *URINAL* from the U-Minnesota stadium! It gleamed in clean white porcelain. They had installed a tube (smaller than the usual plumbing) into a retaining jug which held maybe 6 quarts. From that, another wider tube lead through the wall and formed a spout above the piss-trough. There was a valve assembly; they intended to fill the catch jug, then flip the valve and dump the whole gallon and a half on me at once. I thought it was beautiful. Mace did too; it had been his idea.

In a flash I stripped off my jeans, and stood in my well-filled jockstrap. Mace pawed the front of me, admiring the dark blue elastic. Dean Cordell's jockstrap, a beautiful, glorious memorial to my Piss-Daddy. He opened his own slacks. "Man, I been holding since 6:30... fuck I gotta go! Ready?"

"Hey man, it's YOUR rules... the first one should be public, the guys should watch. Call them and drink more, force yourself to drink more while they gather. If you're full enough, you'll be able to do it. I got poppers..." He smiled.

"I wore this jock for *you*, man. OK... Let's get 'em!" He went to the staircase to call, but there was already a troop of Deltas on the way down. Johann lead the way; but he saw Mace's jeans opened and his dick ready to perform and was a bit put out.

"Hey, I thought I was going to go first?" It was an assumption only he had made, but his opinion was always the only one that mattered. To him anyway.

"Well, I got the honor. Only one who ranks me in this house is Barlow."

At that Barlow said, "Nope, you go ahead man. I'll be ready to join in just a minute." The guys gathered around quickly and I was hemmed in. I had to get in the tub. It was time.

Mace stepped up to the edge, his pants were already opened at the top. He tugged the front open and they fell almost to his knees. Several of the frat brothers kind of ooh'ed at the sight of him as he pulled his equipment out the side of his sweaty, full jockstrap. Apparently they had never seen the golden fur on him, let alone the big thick veiny dick he presented. I knelt, waiting for him to show me how he wanted it. He took a big gulp of his beer, then I handed him the poppers.

"What's that?" one of the guys asked, and someone was explaining it when Mace suddenly thrust forward and let loose, the hot stream suddenly gushing out. He sprayed me on my chest, onto my jock and then in my face. I opened my mouth to give him a target. The men cheered.

"Yeah man, get it in there!" "Yeah that's it, take it bitch!" "Ho, drink him down faggot, come on!" I gulped a mouthful, then leaned forward, wide open. I reached up and grabbed Bill Macey by his hips, and pulled him forward. He splashed me good as I sucked his dick into my mouth and began nursing. The guys went wild; they no longer saw the stream but knew I was actually taking it. I gulped and guzzled, Mace poured it on.

He was only half done, if that, and Baecker stepped up beside him. "Hey man, HERE!" and as quickly his pants were at his ankles. He pulled open the fly of his tightie-whities and his big, beautiful manhood flopped out for all to see. I could barely glance to the side, but Corcoran and 2 of the 'guests' were close enough and lighted enough I could easily tell their cocks were rock hard in their pants. Johann flipped his cock up and down, showing it off, then his slit flared and he began to pour piss on me too.

I reached up and took hold of his shaft, still sucking on Mace. Baecker put his arm around Mace's middle and moved close. He stopped his stream as he lined up beside Bill and was trying to slide his dick into my mouth. I clenched Bill's tube and stopped the flow, then maneuvered then both into my mouth. Releasing my pressure, I was overwhelmed with TWO full piss streams charging into my gullet at once. I thought I would choke, but somehow, my glottis opened and I wasn't swallowing, but their piss was shooting straight down my esophagus in a hot, hard torrent. It didn't occur to me that this was exactly what Carl had done in his scene at the LoadingZone, but I still have no idea how it actually works.

"Oh my fuckin' *GOD!*" I thought, and simply let myself slide into a trance, a heaven of piss pleasure as they filled me. Bill's stream began to taper, then stop, and he was drawing back. Already though Bill Barlow was there to take his place. Then Gordie and Mike Tollefson... they were lined up. Barlow had on a pair of twill pants and had only his penis sticking through the fly. He wasn't ready to show off the whole picture. He waited until Johann was finishing, grunting and carrying on an obscene torrent.

"Yeah faggot, that's it man, DRINK that big cock! That's it you cocksucker, take it down yeah *drink me* man yeah fucker, *take it*..." At last his stream dwindled and he finished with a spurt and drew back. There were plenty of admiring comments and back slapping for him; his little claque worshipped him properly and he felt like a star. But his cock *was* beautiful, there was no denying that. And damn he'd given me his *PISS!* I was already feeling the volume in my belly.

Tollefson had taken his pants off, and stood in his undies. He wore Jockey's 'jeans' briefs, blue and made to look like denim complete with yellow stitching. A good sized spot told me of his oozing, but his dick was pudgy and short; not at all hard. He too flipped down the waistband and pushed his whole basket forward. His bush was thick, sweaty and very pungent. He took hold of my head in his hands and pulled me onto him, forcing his dick as far in as he could, making up for size in force. My nose buried in his fur and I swooned in the manly scent.

It wasn't a real nice smell, but wild and animal, redolent of testosterone and sweat. He paused a moment, I waited. He made loud grunting and face fucking moves, but nothing came forth. I simply let him work on me, then he drew back with a fake-satisfied, "Ahhhhh!" I said nothing; I didn't want to embarrass him. I knew he'd perform later. Then Gordie stepped up and pulled the front of his jeans open.

He too sported a nice spunky jockstrap, and pulled his whole basket out the side. His balls and sac were furry, very hairy, although the trail leading up his belly was not all that thick. He smelled nice, fine and manly. I reached up and took him in. Instantly his bladder pulsed and the piss flowed.

I guzzled fast, taking it down. But again I wasn't able to keep up with the volume. I snorted out my nostrils and again the boys cheered in horny merriment. I had to drop his cock and he pissed on my body and into my face as I tried to catch my breath. I recovered in time to take the last third of his load. His piss was rich, very golden and tasty. He spurted into my mouth once, twice and as quickly as he'd started he was done and stepped back with a grin.

"WHOA! Damn that was HOT! Damn man, I never knew pissing on someone would be so HOT!" He slid his jeans the rest of the way off and cast them aside, and in his jockstrap headed to refill his beer mug.

Bill Barlow was next.

Just as Mike had done, Barlow held my head and slowly slipped his cock into my mouth. He was calm, relaxed and self assured. His smooth abdomen was taut, pushed forward and I knew he was not pudgy; this one would be a FULL load as well. He leaned back, his buddy Corcoran bracing him and reaching around to steady us all. A spurt, then a gush, then...

Piss.

Oh fuck, Barlow had hot, steaming strong golden PISS. In an instant I knew this was a treat and nursed as fast and deeply as I could, making sure I would take him all. He pulled back a bit, and slid in and out of my mouth as he drained. It was golden, heavenly. He pissed.

I once more reached up to caress his balls, holding him and trying to stanch the flow a bit. He wasn't having it though, and pushed my hand away and PISSED as hard as he could. I clenched my eyes closed and tried to manage, but horked piss up and out my nose. There was an instant cheer among the men.

"Yeah Bill! Show him about it! Give it to him!" I didn't try to back off, but gulped and inhaled, forced it up and out my nose all at the same time. My nostrils burned, my sinuses were coated and partly filled with that rank, golden liquid. I began to swoon a bit, but kept on. The tickling of piss in my trachea and lungs worried me, but I held it together.

Barlow shot more and more into me, then finally his stream began to lessen. He spurted, gave a few more, then paused. One more hot burst shot across my tongue and he was done. Corcoran pulled him back and then smooched him quickly on his neck; Barlow looked highly embarrassed but no one said anything. Then Corcoran stepped around to the front. I was gripping the rim of the tub, trying to catch my breath and hacking, gagging and coughing piss out of my throat and sinuses. I heard steps plunking on the plywood platform behind me. One, two guys were up there, getting ready to play with the hardware we'd installed.

Corcoran also had taken his pants completely off and strutted up to me in his boxers. He pulled his equipment out the fly; big LOW hanging balls and plenty of hair, medium sized uncut cock half-hard flopping before me. He lifted his dick for me to take it in my mouth, intending something horrible, but thank God I got a full whiff of it before I tasted it. I turned abruptly aside.

"No fuckin' way! Give me a BEER!" He paused, a bit unsure what to do. Mace had a big stein ready and offered it to me. I took a big swig, then addressed them all. "I'm not taking the cheese off THAT thing. Here, let me wipe you down and I'll continue. I'm not sucking that spunk off your dick man, no way." He smiled a bit, almost proud of himself, but let me take his dick and splash beer on him, pulling his nasty foreskin back. I washed him in it, letting it slop down on me, and into the tub. In a minute I had him ready. He too had quite the pronounced swelling in his abdomen and I knew he held plenty.

I wasn't wrong. I barely got his 5" into my mouth and it opened. A slow stream of nasty tasting piss gushed into my mouth and I almost choked. Vitamins; I'm sure he hadn't thought of it, and truthfully neither had I. In my limited experience, I'd never encountered a piss-feeder who'd had such a dose in his system. But I forced myself to keep going and take him. As I myself often do, he thickened and got harder while he pissed and I nursed from him. By the time I'd taken a quarter of his load, he had a full-tilt hard-on. His cockhead was at the back of my throat, and he pumped, forced, gushed into me. He PISSED and poured, gushed his juice into my mouth and his hot hard dick jumped and swelled as he fed me.

His stream tapered and waned, he spurted a few more blasts into my tonsils, but made no effort to pull back. He was easily the most loaded of the men so far, it still being fairly early, and he was going for more than draining. I slurped and sucked on him and in a few seconds it was apparent to the others this was more than pissing. Some weren't real happy about it.

"Hey Cork! Get the hell back outta there man! You go for that later on! It's MY Turn!" and the like. One of his buddies, another alumnus, took him by the shoulder and pulled him back away from me. His hard cock popped out with a slurp and there was once more a general 'OOOH!' when the others saw a full-bored, honest to god _Hard-On_ in that roomfull of 'straight' men. He was protesting being taken away.

"Man, lemme finish! He's gonna take our cum too! I wanna bust a nut!"

I smiled, the others were cheering and laughing. I could've taken the break at this point and done him but there were still more than 20 guys to drain... They weren't willing to wait. The men on the platform were laughing and I turned to see what they were doing. I heard a stream of piss shooting into the urinal above me and knew they were loading up the first douche from their set-up for me. Then another and another; 3 or 4 guys pissed their loads into the porcelain and filled the holding jug. But in front of me...

Two more Deltas stood in their shorts. Both had rather smallish dicks, but slim bodies and complimentary forms. One blond, one dark. One hairy, one smooth. One blue eyed, one brown... and they posed almost facing each other as they sidled up to the edge of the tub; they'd seen Johann's stunt and wanted to do a double again. I was ready.

I motioned them and got into position. I took both cocks into my lips together. From their size and our position, I was able to get just the dickheads, but had a nice suction on them. They held each other up, arms around their waists, giggling a bit drunkenly. "C'mon Tommy let's do it!" the one laughed, but it was his buddy who opened first. I sucked and drank.

His piss dribbled into my mouth, spurt drip drip drip, spurt drip drip drip, then stopped. Then Tommy gave me a jolt. He spewed a nice solid stream for 3 or 4 seconds, then dribbled off. Then the first again. then Tommy. It went on alternately for minutes, making it hot and wonderful, easy to do them both. Theirs was thin, beer piss. It was almost foamy in itself. My belly was filling; I'd already taken about 8 cups of man-piss, almost 2 quarts. There was a long, long way to go.

Above me the 4 had finished pissing in the urinal. The motioned to some others as the holding tank was only a third filled. I heard one saying, "Damn it looks like fuckin' water; you sure you guys PISSED in there?" I figured (rightly it turned out,) that it was the volume they were most interested in, piss yes, but they augmented the jug with beer. They didn't want to dilute it too much, and neither did I really, and they were trying to get a few of the others to help them fill it for the first round with the flood of piss from the pipe.

Three more guys went up the platform to help out and suddenly there were at least 6 in front of me. The beer keg was doing its work on the guys and the urge was hitting a whole group at once. They jockied into positions, pants open, pants down, pants off, jockstraps and briefs, boxers and naked flesh... hard dicks, soft cocks, medium dicks, large dicks, manflesh and phalluses of all descriptions; it was beautiful. I let them push and jostle each other and simply opened my mouth. Those who could insert themselves did so, others pissed on and into me from back a bit.

On the pissing went, men I didn't recognize filled me, two guys in what I thought were red union-suits approached and pulled fat stubby dicks from behind the flaps. Their piss was hot and thick, stinking like the piss of a truck stop urinal, a gas station trough. I leaned back and let my eyes droop as load after load was offered.

I drank them when they wanted it, I drank until I was in another reality.

Events seemed to be in a kind of slow motion; but things happened so fast I barely had time to take notice. A high-speed slow motion, almost seeing the action from a corner of the ceiling. I mused that I might actually, literally be, beside myself. I wished I was; I'd enjoy seeing myself feasting on all that cock and sucking piss out of these wild college boys. The creaking and thumping above me became intense, and I could hear streams of piss splashing in against the porcelain. The man in front of me shoved his cock into my mouth and I gulped, trying to turn my head to see who was on the platform.

He reached around and pulled me back. "Hey man, DRINK IT! That's what this is all about bitch! Take my PISS, fucker!" I didn't know him at all; one of the guests? Someone from campus? Had they unlocked the doors upstairs? I had no idea and didn't really care.

Johann returned, clad in his briefs only. His big, firm body gleamed, slick and wet. I wondered why the others would be wet, were they playing too? Was someone else, *Johann* for god's sake, taking piss from my scene? Nah, but maybe they were getting crazy and someone had poured beer on him. Still, piss wasn't beyond reality at that point. The men were wild...

Baecker's manhood bulged nicely in the snug, damp white fabric, his cock pointing up, curved and thick. The arcs of his balls at the lower edge, the bugle of dick reaching up, up into his belly was a vision of masculine attraction. He came up to the trough again, a liter-mug all but empty in his hand.

"Hey lil' buddy, how's it going? You getting enough from the MEN there you lil' faggot?" He grinned, getting to the floaty-drunk stage. He was fine, having a great time. "You need another load from *this* fat dick faggot?"

I grinned and stroked another Delt who was pissing a pallid, pitiful steam onto me, dribble dribble dribble dribb... Johann knew I wasn't impressed, neither was he. Maybe it was shaped like a dick, maybe the guy had a 'Y' chromosome and testicles, but Johann didn't think that was enough. This was a little boy, giggly sand-box punk wee-wee'ing where he shouldn't. Oh well, I didn't care, and Baecker was ready for round 2.

"Get outta there Phil, lemme SHOW ya what this is all about!" and he flopped the front of his Jockies open, letting his glorious stuff hang out for the punk to see. Once more I watched in rapt awe as he stroked his dick and then leaned in close to offer it to me. Joe-Joe Jones, on the platform, called to him.

"He Johann! We need one more big load up here! Help fill this thing and we're gonna give the piggie a bath! Come on!" John looked at them in contempt; while contemptuous of being 'lead' into anything, he really was enjoying the intimacy, the pure horny beauty of giving his cock, his manly juice, that Essence in his *piss*, to another man, me. He'd had cocksuckers all his life no doubt. Being totally absorbed in his own masculinity, his phallic state knew no end. If someone wanted to respect, to receive, to worship his DICK, he could find time and place for it. And in this public spectacle, this orgy of testosterone and urine, he was in his element.

"Fuck that man, this guy needs my cock in his MOUTH, don't ya Matt? My lil' fag buddy wants me..." He pondered a moment. "The bath huh? They gonna dump that gusher on you huh?" I snickered.

"Yeah it's about time for that too..." I was going into another state, the sudden intake of so much fluid, coupled with beer and smoke and the overdose of hormones and stress had me wildly altered as well. I liked it; I was a urinal, a piss-drinker, a shower-pig, a piss-pig... This scene was making Carl's little 'initiation' look like a playground dare.

[My mind unhitched from the 'present,' and I saw Carl, Warren and Marky J as adolescents on a summer day...

"Yeah Carl, I dare ya. I DARE YA, I double dog DARE YA to suck it and drink some. Here!" Little-boy Warren's hairless dick pulsed and shot piss on little-boy Carl, who in fear and desire, let him wet him, then in force of will, TASTED, drank Warren's *potty*... Little-boy Marky grinned.

"Yeah Marky, I told you he'd do it! You owe me a buck!" he called as he shot his piss onto Carl's face and body. "I told you!"]

The room came back.

"I told you he'd do it!" Bill Barlow was bringing in reinforcements from upstairs. They were laughing and gulping beer. "Hey buddy, here you go, ready for MORE?"

"Wait yer damn turn," John said. "You didn't answer. Do YOU want to drink from my dick Matt, or want us to go up and fill the jug?"

My reverie had ended; I reached for Johann's beautiful manly equipment. "Here man, lemme suck you," I muttered. "Send them others up..." John grinned and put his hands on the sides of my head, pulling my face up to his cock.

"You heard him, you guys go piss in the pot! This fag needs my dick in his mouth..."

ROUND TWO

PURGATORY

Barlow and his companions tromped onto the wooden steps, up onto the platform. John held me gently, almost tenderly as he let his dick jump and then... opened. His urethra opened to me.

Piss. Oh god, Johann's piss...

He pissed. Suddenly I was back in the present, the here, the now. I was sucking John Baecker and he was feeding me *Piss*. Oh god, what the hell was I doing? My belly was full, almost distended.

I gulped and forced myself to take it. I slugged and swallowed, and he slurped down the last ounces of beer from his mug. "Yeah Matt, that's it. Drink the beer-piss, show me you like sucking that dick buddy. Yeah!" His eyes were glazed. He was now floating, heading into that sexual, pheromone-filled land of manly scents and hard cocks, of marked bushes and sloppy jeans, of sweaty, crusty jockstraps and j/o buddies, the rites of the locker room, of comparing dicks with the other guys and finding *he* was the champ, the top dog, the Alpha... and he pissed for me.

But it was far beyond adolescent weenie-waggling. He shoved his penis to me, letting me use and enjoy, work and worship him in phallic adoration. This was potent, sexual and fulfilling. It was a transference of power, of essence, of manhood. It was orgasm in surrogacy, the hot, manly *piss* making up for the concentrated essence of semen by sheer volume. And John knew all this by instinct, as did I. He pissed, and his cock thickened, hardened in my mouth. The intoxicating, obsessive nature of man-piss possessed us, sent us. We were linked in the bizarre, hot sexual union of *piss*.

Above me, the splashing continued as 4 drunken men pissed together, the beautiful porcelain urinal catching their piss, channeling it to the jug and holding it, holding it for me. Johann's piss slackened, his hands still holding my face and feeding me slowly, sensuously. He slacked, the stream tapered off, dribbled and ended. His erection irrefutably testified to his power, his lust in piss too.

He looked up to the men behind the little wooden wall.

"Yeah let's get that ready Bill!" he said. Barlow laughed and finished his pissing. I turned and saw the way he was looking down at the guy beside him, watching that stream flow, spurt and splash in the white unit. His fascinated glaze was beautiful, and I was all but sure he was reaching beside him, holding his buddy's penis and *helping* him, helping him to piss. The jug was full, and they wanted to see this...

Johann snapped out of his homosexual union with me and stepped to the end of the tub. Backing away, he tucked his cock back into his white shorts. The union was broken, he denied me the 'more.' He could see the men atop the platform and me beneath the set-up. The pipe was pointing into the tub, in the center, about a foot up from the rim. Baecker motioned to me to take it.

Barlow and the others came back down to witness the scene, only Dave Carlton remained, to work the valve. The others gathered around and called to the men in the room.

"Hey it's time for the piggie's BATH!" they yelled, and 10-12 drunken frat boys stumbled up, laughing, oohing and ahhing, hot and ready for the next level of depravity in piss. Bill and Johann were side by side, their smirks made me a bit self-conscious. The union, the unspoken link we'd had moment before was gone, replaced with his pride, his contempt. He sneered. I knew it was his defense, he couldn't ever acknowledge the obsession, the needs of his own homosexuality. But it was painful nonetheless. If he'd but smiled, cheered me in piss-lust or encouragement I would've been sent into a new and beautiful realm of that trans-dimensional place, that testosterone-charged land of *Piss*. But he sneered, mocking me, mocking what we'd just shared.

They were animals, ugly and vile, wild and mean, and Johann pushed me toward the tube. It was plastic, about 1½ inch across, thick and heavy, leading up to the holding tank. He laughed, "Get ready faggot, you're gonna get some piss now!" He lifted the end of it and pushed my face toward it; I took it in my mouth.

Barlow stumbled and almost fell and the others sent up a cheer, "Open it, give it to him!" and Carlton yanked the lever, flipped the knob or whatever it was. There was a moment of gravity, of air and then an incredible, indescribable torrent of lukewarm foamy PISS blasted into my face. It whelmed me, gushing and pouring. I drank, gulped and swallowed, but the greater part of it by far simply blasted past my face, over my body and down my chest.

The disembodied piss gushed and flew, exploded around me, a cloud of insanity and horny elation. I was plunged into a sea of bizarre needs and even more bizarre fulfillments, of psychosis on an incredible level, of perversion and a damaged nature set literally on a platform and shown for all to see. I was disgusted, horrified, and loathed myself in a way I'd never known before.

I closed my eyes and tried to swallow. I thought I would vomit. I was bathed in clammy piss and it pooled in the tub, around my knees. My dick and balls shrivelled in my jock, Dean's fine blue jock. I was wet and cold, stinking and perverse. Tears welled up as the shotgunning piss finally ran its course and stopped, the last of it falling like a yellow bolt into the tub. The last drips from the tube were a twisted parody of the droplets of semen in a piss-slit after orgasm. I was a *faggot*, a piss faggot and I hated it, hated myself.

The fraternity men screamed in wild disgust, loving the perversity of the scene. My eyes swelled hot and bitter, and I fought to control the outburst I felt immanent. I gulped, my stomach aching in its abusive overload of urine, beer and bodily fluids. My belly stuck forward. I looked malformed, bizarre, distended. Pregnant... impregnated with the output of dozens of hateful, vile men, inferior to me in every way yet able to put *Me* into this subjugation of need and humiliation. Faggot! Oh god, a *piss faggot*, how the fuck did it come to this?

A hot tear began to run down my cheek and Rocky Rockne pushed Gustavson toward me. They were both down to their shorts, Rockne's hairy belly almost as swollen as mine, filled with beer. Gus' dick was shrivelled, cold and tiny, but he wasn't concerned. Rocky's hot phallus was tumescent, blue veins running thickly up and down the shaft. His white skin glowed, the fine golden hair glinting in the bluish light of the room. They reached for me.

"Hehehe, yeah man! We wanna do the double! C'mon Gus, let's fill the faggot!" Once more I was crushed in the humiliation. I'd worked hard, made sacrifices to help Gus get through Calculus; almost as much as Johann's repudiation of me, his contempt wounded me, stung me bitterly.

"Wait a minute, damn... you can't piss in him with *that* little thing! C'mon bitch, get him woke up, suck that dick and get him ready!" He roughly pushed his buddy toward me, and Gus laughed as he ripped his shorts down, stepping out of them, standing naked and proud. I looked in horror at his tiny, pusillanimous dickhead, that little nipple of my disgrace. He reached to the back of my neck and yanked me close, mashing his sweaty little dick on my cheek.

He adjusted and I got the head into my mouth and began sucking him in resignation. It was a hell, a purgatory, the weight of shame all but fatal. I wanted simply to die in that tub, leaving the horrible tableau of my wrecked body and shattered psyche flung aside in a pool of piss. I deserved nothing better. Throw me in the toilet, literally this TOILET, this urinal, and walk away. Laughter rang around me, echoing and mocking me the more. The shame, the unremitting shame... and there was no way out. This was going to continue. How long, who could say?

Gustavson's cock responded quickly. His little knob pushed farther and farther into my mouth, until his full 6.5" was extended. The quintessential 'grower,' his penis was nothing to be embarrassed about; he was a fine Nordic man, and _he_ was not the one kneeling naked in a jockstrap, sucking the piss out of all and sundry, dozens of strangers. Another tear began to run from my eye and he laughed.

"Aw the little faggot is gonna CRY! Hahahahaha! No shit, you fuckin' bitch! C'mon Rocky let's give the fuck something to cry ABOUT!" and they took my head and forced both their hot cocks into my mouth. I was too crushed, too vile to resist, to protest. It would've done no good anyhow, I'd written my own damnation, made my own hell. Why should THEY care?

Tears ran down my face and I waited in that trough, that toilet. I was a toilet boy, a pig, a piss-pig faggot. They laughed, mocked and then pissed.

Piss. More piss.

"Jesus what the hell is this?" I thought. "I'm drinking PISS, taking urine from their bodies, their WASTE material, and drinking it. Oh Jesus Christ!" I wasn't meaning to pray, but I pleaded silently, "_God help me... Help..._"

Both cock slits opened and the two men held each other, laughing insanely and letting their cocks rub and mix in my mouth. The weenie-rubbing, the tentative touching of penis to penis of the lockerroom on a new scale, but the experiment thrilled them. They pissed together and tried to see who could piss harder, deeper. It shot from my mouth around them and they howled in pride and contempt.

"Hahaha, yeah take it fucker! Fuckin' fag! Hahaha, yeah go Gus, give it to him!"

"Hehe, fuck Rocky you got some pee there man! Go for it! Do it, man!" I drowned, my inner being dying in shame. The *men*, they would never ever see me as anything but a toilet again. Nor would I, it seemed.

Piss ran down me, and I tried vainly to gulp, to swallow and drink it all. What else was I good for? Fuck it, drink them, I'd said I would, why did I say that if I wasn't going to DO it, if I was worth anything more than this insane scene? I drank, my belly hurting more and the force of impending regurgitation made me swoon. Their streams tapered, mercifully soon they were done. They pulled back and out, spurting their last few bursts of piss onto my body, into my face. They laughed.

"Pig!"

I collapsed onto the floor of the tub, wallowing in several inches of cold piss and spilled beer. Silently the tears ran and burned my face. I didn't want the men to see it, but several others stepped up to laugh and mock, mock me in my deepest disgrace and utter shame. Why shouldn't they? *Dis-grace:* no grace, no finesse, no humanity left. Just animalian filth, wallowing in piss.

I saw Kent there, my piss-buddy and swimming pal. He had gotten me into this, it was as if he'd known the destruction, the depths it would lead to. I didn't know how my friend, a kind of *lover*, could do this to me. His piss had been wonderful, something private we shared. Our obsession with piss and jockstraps was now ripped open, bared for all to see and mock. I was dying.

Two of the brothers came up, a full pitcher in their hands. They giggled and talked, and I knew damn well it wasn't beer. The gaggle of men they were standing among at the side of the room watched as they offered it, expecting me to chug it down. I slurped from the edge of it, then the taller one grabbed it and upended it on my head, into my face. They screamed in laughter. The plastic pitcher clattered into the tub. I slowly pushed it up and aside, away.

Bill Barlow had his arm around yet another newcomer, and now I knew they were setting me up, taking my humiliation far beyond the limits we'd agreed. Fair and mocha, he was nevertheless black, a NEGRO, and my mind shattered as his smooth, slick brown skin blocked out the sight of anything else. There were no black men in this chapter of Delta Tau.

He was a god, black and fine, his naked flesh wrapped in a stark white *Jockstrap*. I was on the verge of fainting as he pulled me upright, holding me as gently and sensuously as Johann had, even moreso.

His fat, thick purple cock was uncut, but he was clean, redolent of fresh showering, not soap but clean skin, his fragrant bush nappy and scratchy as he mashed his penis into my mouth. I wanted to scream, to protest, but an unseen force compelled me and somehow I even *smiled* as I opened up and let him use me, making me _his_ urinal too.

That moment of anticipation was an absolute Hell; but then his *Piss* coursed into my mouth and onto my tongue, and once more the Power of my obsession was restored. It was sweet, thick and yellow, hot *Piss*, hotter than anyone's had been so far. He wasn't fevered but this was not 98.6 degrees. It scalded me in beauty and joy, and I drank him deliciously.

"Yeah go for it Tiger!" the guys were cheering. "Give it to him!" Barlow, Carlton, Baecker and Corcoran watched as he filled me. Rocky and Gus looked on uncomprehendingly. My guts were strained to the limit. Tiger touched my head, holding me gently and spoke low, softly.

"Yeah bro, yeah... goddam buddy, yeah, that's it. You the man, you can do it. Ah, yeah Matt take it now, you got it!" He pissed for me, pissed in me and gave me himself. I took power from him, and it was as if the world again opened, a golden plane of reality, a new reality. I might have been dreaming, but it was a hyper-reality and I received him in joy.

ROUND THREE

EPIPHANY

The self-deprecation of mere moments before was blasted away in a flash, an epiphany. Tiger let his manly juice flow, pissing and filling me. The pain of rejection, of humiliation was replaced with a kind of pride, a self-awareness and glory few men ever achieve.

Johann watched from the sidelines, his beautiful body slick and wet, his Jockey shorts plump with his masculinity. But could he do what I'd done? What I would yet _Do_ this night? No way... and not by lack of endurance, by physical weakness...

Rather by weakness of mind and soul. The weakness of a hot, homosexual man trapped in the expectations, trapped by the burdens of social stigma and guilt. He would never be able to enjoy the real, true sharing of masculine sex, no matter how many men he pumped sperm, pounded his cock and even piss into. _Fear_. His fear would forever deny him the beauty of truly _Sharing_ his nature with another, an equal, someone _The Same_ as himself.

Despite the moment of beautiful sex, of _union_ we'd just accomplished, he'd missed the point. My belly ached, strained to the limit of capacity as I took more and more piss from the hot black man. I drank, and he _did_ understand what I was doing, what I was accomplishing, and acknowledged that he in fact could _not_.

I was transformed.

If I drank and drank piss until my body literally exploded, it was not a weakness that caused it, rather strength. I could kill myself in piss, in sex, because I had the _power_, the sheer masculine _Power_ to know and understand the beauty, the obsession of the Penis and Piss. Of semen and copulation, of need and desire fulfilled. I drank and my eyes cleared.

It was as if that urination went on for a day, two... Tiger pissed and his hot, sweet elixir filled me, the strain in my belly no longer painful. As I'd done when Dean raped me, I forced myself past an unseen line, and pain transcended into something beyond. It was still 'pain,' but it was something more, something higher, glorious and strange.

Insane? Try to explain it rationally, these punks would never be able to come to terms with it. Never. Not giving, not taking, not experiencing the sheer power of being able to insert one's masculine nature into another; to give and share as only men can. To penetrate and fill, to be penetrated and be filled, to explore a man's body from inside out, to be explored, known; and to nurse, feed from one another in hot sexual congress.

Humiliating? Hardly, for I knew myself, knew the power and the need. Knew the desire and how to sate it. Knew the Obsession and its fulfillment. I knew the object and the subject, the beginning and the end, the Alpha and the Omega. Do you suppose those forces are absent from others, simply because they cannot explain, cannot understand and express the inner nature of them? The dark, unseen desire of a man to find his Equal, his Likeness, his _Homo_...

I was a _homo_ and I loved it. I loved the men, their cocks, their bodies; I loved their piss and masculine power as I fed from it.

I loved myself.

If they parted with their essence and filled me without awareness of its _value_, of its meaning, so much the worse for their pitiable, truly childish sexuality. I took it, and raised that nature and myself onto a new, glorious plane. Oh I could feed them too; I can fuck, I can fill and violate and invade, explore and know them too. But in this moment, I received it all, the scent, the liquid, the food of the _Gods_! I drank _Piss_ and in a way I stole, robbed them of their masculinity in being their bitch.

From a heap of wet, destroyed pigmeat in the toilet to a powerful, transcendent sex-god, I rose up proud and magnificent, and drank Tiger's piss. His flow, thick and hot, tapered and waned, and I sucked hard, taking it, demanding it, forcing him to give me his utmost. I drank his last drops and he backed away, over-whelmed by the experience. I think he too felt everything that had just blasted through my consciousness, and it not only cowed him, it frightened him. He fed me his COCK and his essence as my due, my Right. He didn't _dare_ refuse me.

He pulled back and looked at me in awe, in wonder. "Yeah man, goddam..." he whispered. "Fuckin' ay..."

I knelt upright, wet and hot, proud... a God. The laughing, mocking men perceived something wild, weird, something profound had just taken place and the jeering abruptly stopped. Gordie came up and looked curiously. My belly stuck out, the straining of my innards apparent from the stretched, distended skin of my hairy body. If I split wide open that second, the sheer power of _Piss_ would lift me up, and as if giving birth to myself in golden heat, I would be reborn.

I could have lifted my legs and spread myself and given them all my asshole just as wildly, just as violently as Dean had fucked me. I could've taken them on, every goddam one of them, and then walked away sneering at _them_ for the power, the strength and total masculinity of it all. The fucking Dean had given me now made perfect sense: in that mind-wrenching, ass-ripping violence, being raped and subjected to his penis, to his Need, to his _Cock_, I had become more a man than ever. And it had not faded, this simply put a finishing touch on the power and glory he had given to me.

Rather had _revealed_ to me; for it was mine by Nature, mine by right and Essence. I was a man, homo and fine. Glorious. Dean had given me nothing I didn't already have.

I had to be destroyed to be reborn. I had to die in piss and humiliation to find my inner power, my obsession with Being, with my own existence and strength. Yes my need, my hunger, but my ability to sate that even for myself, and I don't mean just by drinking my own piss in desperation.

But by finding in the nature of Man he who can fulfill, feed and fit with me, to augment and create that supreme Duality that can only exist in a homo (_alike_) —sexual union of the flesh and the soul at once. So many needy men seek and seek, trying to find that connection, that fit, and never succeed. They take sex as sex only, a bodily function and release, as did Johann. The glory and power that could've been his was lost, and I took it from him.

A woman could only be probed, explored and taken; and given until the end of Time itself will never, ever experience the sublime Power and majesty of _Knowing_ another human being in that way. And a man unable to realize, unable to function in this way too: _THAT_ is a bitch, a cunt. Call me what you like, fuck it. _Faggot_ became a term of Power and glory; anyone who would use that word in contempt was simply too dense, too obtuse to bother with.

I rose in majesty, a God.

Tiger stepped away and I lifted myself up, straining to make my belly hurt more, trying to make myself split asunder. My eyes darted about in a gleam of insanity, hyper-sanity, an awareness beyond words. I stood up tall, stretching to my full height and tilting my head back, and let my guts press upward.

An incredible fountain of man-piss shot up, up and out from my mouth. The men shouted in confusion, in lust, in laughter, in accomplishment. They thought it my demise, that the weight of piss-service had crushed me. I heaved again, forced it up and let it flow down my body, into the tub. Far from it; I was ready, ready for MORE.

"Come on man! WHO'S NEXT?" I called, standing in wet and golden pride, Dean's jockstrap proving my power. I stood defiant and proud. Piss was my crown, gold beyond the gold of Ophir. I was a *piss-drinker*, I embraced it and I loved it.

Piss.

———————————

Men came and went, they drank beer and soda pop, they smoked and came to the trough to feed me. I drank them all, I would waste not a single drop. It was mine, mine to consume, to use or wear or worship as I chose. *They* had agreed too; I drank their piss and they would <u>not</u> deny me. Tollefson and Barlow, Corkie and Tiger, Tommy, Billy, Dave and Mike... Jim and Stan and Rocky and all of them. If there was a man present in that house, he came and gave me his cock and his Piss.

Having heaved up that first bellyful, I knew I could now go on without fear of hydro-intoxication. Piss has a lot of the enzymes the body needs anyway; but I'd known coming into the scene that water intoxication can be fatal. More than one frat party or hazing has resulted in someone dying from a sudden intake of so much fluid. Throwing up was a safety valve as well... it was the *action* of drinking the men, not holding the liquid, which was the point.

I called to Kent, and made him come up and give me his dick. I'd been wanting more of him for hours and I insisted he feed me. As in so many instances in the locker-room, the dorm, my apartment, it was the unique, silent union of his cock and my gullet, his piss and my need. His manly juice filling my body with strength and lust. I drank him, pawed him and gulped it down. He was amazed, frightened. He was another who, knowing only the one side of the equation could not fathom the other.

I told Gordie to roll me a smoke and fetch another bottle of poppers. I took a minute break, loudly proclaiming that the men would WAIT for me, wait to give me their fluids. There was a murmur of those left standing, more than half the fraternity having fallen by the wayside. I smoked a bit and resumed, drinking another four men in quick succession. Then for only the second time, Bill Macey came up.

"Mace, man... man, where ya been?" I asked, the gleam in my eye insane, powerful and wild. He nodded, his pants long gone and he strutted proudly in his jockstrap. That solidarity with me spoke volumes, he wanted to join with me again.

I offered him the poppers and he let me stroke and tug him, getting his dick hot and hard as his belly showed its fullness. I took him in my mouth, the union private and fine, the others no longer paying attention. I suckled and pawed him, then spoke.

"Give it to me man, let me take you..." I murmured. He smiled, his own need clear and apparent. He let his penis stand forth in beauty and I sucked as he huffed the poppers and let his stream flow. Once more, I drank from his beautiful hose, my body taking his fluid in horny joy. He pissed, spurted and pissed. I drank fast and hard, gulping and sucking it down. I'd stopped trying to control anyone's flow, rather took as I could and let the rest shoot out the sides of my mouth, up and out my nose, down my body. I didn't care.

My own belly again was stretched, full and distended. I loved it as I sucked from Mace, taking him into my Being. He flowed, gave himself to me and I reached around, feeling his asshole. His self-consciousness was overcome by testosterone and drink; his buzz allowing him to accept, to open to my probing even in the middle of the room. His eyes rolled back, closed and I reached into him, my finger feeling his rectum, his prostate. He bucked and pissed.

In slow minutes he filled me, drained himself and then stopped. He looked down at me and I noticed sunlight gleaming in from one of the basement windows. It was well into Saturday morning. Mace touched my face, my sticky, sodden face. I was coated with dried and drying piss from more than 30 men. He glanced about the room, nobody conscious was present, and he leaned down to kiss me. The ordeal was over; maybe I'd find one more man to piss for me, in me, but it was over.

Mace tugged at me and said, "Man, come on... this was WILD!" I finally stepped from the tub, my damp feet shocked at the feeling of cold concrete rather than wet porcelain. My jockstrap was sticky, thick and fine. Piss. I was a Piss God. Mace loved me...

I walked to the side of the room and sat on one of the stools. I surveyed the scene, god it must've been _something!_ I was proud, awesome in accomplishment. Mace stood with me, saying nothing. We were the last two standing.

"Mace, man... you ready?" He didn't get it.

"Huh?"

"You wanna fuck? Come on man, let me have you... I need you man. I want your asshole. I need your _asshole_. I wanna fuck you man. You wanna taste MY piss?"

The two of us embraced, alike, the same. In our full jockstraps and horny flesh, we were one being, _homo_.

He wanted me to fuck him again, for sure. He looked around. "Oh man... _where_?"

"Well, your room? We're not going all the way over to my place man..."

"Um, I think a couple of the guys from Eau Claire are up in my room. Last I saw, it was taken." I was nonplussed.

"Then right here man, I want you. I'm going to fuck you Mace..." I said softly. The horny idea was OK, he didn't care. Whether it was drunkenness or need, it didn't matter even if we might be discovered. We went to one of the side rooms, a small room with only one chair and a thick rug. I brought the lube and poppers from beside the trough, the piss tub. I held his hand and we walked in silence.

We closed the door and I embraced the fine man, pulling him close and mashing our jockstraps together. His cock bulged, thick and hot, and I pressed on his shoulders to make him drop. He slowly sank to his knees and with closed eyes took my cock from the pouch and began to suck me. His elation was pure, simple and fine. If we'd had time, I could've explained the epiphany of the night to him, he would've understood. Right now, he sucked and I offered him to drink.

"You want to try some Mace? Take my juice?" I whispered.

"Man, oh man I don't know..." His fear was not feigned, nor did he try to hide it. He wasn't ready for that. I sank down on my knees with him, and kissed him slowly, then laid him back.

"It's OK, man, it's OK. Maybe another time, maybe when we're *alone*..." He smiled again, and kissed me deeply.

His furry body tingled as I lubed his asshole and slowly, slowly and gently entered him. We joined, linked, united.

Gently and beautifully I fucked him, the thoughts of knowing and exploring, of penetrating yet completing the masculine *Duality* flowing through my mind. I rejoiced that it was Mace who coupled with me in this moment of epiphany, and as his cock swelled against my belly I felt my balls boiling for release. The pent-up sexuality of the whole night burst forth in power and hot spunk, shooting gobs of my seed deep into his willing receptacle. I groaned softly, the shouting and power of the night abated. Sensuously I came, pumping cum into him for long beautiful seconds.

"Ah, oh god Mace, here! Take it man... ugggghhjh!" I whispered in his ear as I spurted into his asshole, into his guts. In a moment he was with me.

"Oh Matt... FUCK!" he grunted, as he bucked up and shot his sperm between us, spattering up and onto us both. *Union.* I kissed him again, and held him fast, his legs up over my shoulders, wide and open, his asshole filled with my cock. I loved him and without thinking, I let myself relax.

I took another hit of the poppers, slow and gentle, and my valve opened. I pissed up, inside him, pissing and filling him. In a few seconds he felt it too. His eyes opened wide in shock and disbelief, but he made no attempt to move or stop me. His lips parted and once more he closed his eyes, taking me, *receiving* me. I filled him, flooding his guts with piss.

Piss. He was going to learn to love it too.

We drifted in piss-lust until I was finished, then I pulled away, pulled out of him slowly. He clenched his asshole instinctively, and nothing was lost. He stood, ran his hand down his belly, feeling the load within himself. His beautiful oozing cock hung beside his pouch, and he straightened himself. Once more we were alike, *homos*, standing together in our jockstraps and the beauty of post-coital joy. My fluids planted deep in him, as so many beautiful men had filled and fed me. He looked long into my eyes and the unspoken connection united us.

We slipped from the room silently, and back in the main room found our clothing. We dressed and the night was finished. We went upstairs and looked around.

There were 3 or 4 Deltas passed out in chairs, on the couch. Barlow and Corcoran were in the kitchen, making coffee. They looked at the two of us, but had no inkling.

"Hey man, you got through it! You want some coffee?"

I nodded, but added, "I need to puke first. There's no room for coffee in here!" They laughed, and Mace went with me to the hallway bathroom. Looking up the stairs, we saw John Baecker peering over the bannister, bedraggled and confused. Perhaps something of the loss had occurred to him? I neither knew nor cared. He looked at me with something other than contempt, and turned back to his room, confused. Mace and I went into the bathroom together.

"Man, I don't want to do this, but I can't hold it," he said. I nodded and smiled.

"It was the thought, the *idea* of it Mace, it's OK. Let it out." He sat on the toilet and with a gush, he shit my piss out his asshole. It reeked, man-guts and piss mixed in that union. It was pale, thin beer piss, piss distilled from the others' piss, and a big, thick gob of my cum floated atop it all. Unashamedly he spread his legs and we looked into the toilet, admiring our work. I let him finish, then he flushed. He left the room to pour our coffee and I leaned over the bowl. A gush, a rush and I vomited almost a gallon of piss, thin and watery. I looked at it with pride. The essence, the manly *substance* of it remained. Nothing could take that from me.

The four of us had coffee, Barlow about ready to pass out. Corcoran was subdued, embarrassed by his participation, embarrassed by my presence as I sat in the room with them, redolent of piss, and knowing the anatomy, the kink of every one of the fraternity brothers. It was *him* who was the pig, the bitch; not me. He knew it now too. I'd surpassed them all.

I decided to end that party; it was 'over' when I walked out. I made ready to leave. Bill Macey walked me to the door, and with Barlow's keys finally opened the bolt lock. He picked something up from the sideboard table as we went onto the porch together.

"Here Matt, I got something for you..." I paused and turned. He held it up to me. A jockstrap...

A fine Bike jockstrap, the red and black lines of the waist-band highlighting the bright <u>yellow</u> color. A yellow jockstrap, a *Piss-Boy's jockstrap*! The pride that flooded me almost equaled that of the Trough. My Epiphany was completed.

"Aw Mace... thank you man!" I almost shouted. He shushed me and took a quick, secretive look around; there was nobody to see as he gave me a quick kiss on the cheek.

"I got it for you in this sports store downtown man, I thought you'd like it..." He'd known instinctively what it meant! We admired it together, then with one more sly smooch, I stuffed it into my back pocket and turned to go down the steps onto the sidewalk.

I went into the sunny morning, and away from the Delta house. Mace watched me from the window, his body aching with manly pride at our homo-sexual coupling. He knew he was a piss-hound now too, having become my urinal in our hot fucking. If he could take it up the ass, he'd be able to taste and savor, to drink me too.

He knew no one would ever top the events of that night; his own awareness had grown almost as much as mine, he shared the Epiphany. He loved me silently as he watched me walk away.

GRADUATION AND BEYOND

For the next 3 weeks, things were kind of strange on campus. Even though I lived in my own apartment away from the dorms and clubs, the frat houses and student associations, word of *The Party* and my stellar performance had gotten around. Of course it did; how would it not?

Mace laid low, he was too self-conscious and intimidated to be seen with me. Barlow had his own issues to deal with, getting called up on the carpet with the Provost and the Dean of Students to explain what the hell had taken place at the Delta Tau House party. Two representatives from their national association would be visiting to make a 'review,' and it was mentioned that a revocation of their fraternity charter was not out of the question. I simply ignored most of it.

But it was tough to ignore it when groups of arrogant 'heterosexual' men on a street corner howled and cat-called and hooted when I drove past a pizzeria; screaming at me and groping their genitals. "*Hey PISS PIG! I gotta GO MAN, c'mere and DRINK ME, BITCH!*" and so on. Only once did I think it would lead to something beyond name-calling and attempted humiliation: I was at the pool house and three of the Varsity swimmers tried to corner me in the locker room. The steel lockers, tile floors, wooden benches and so on had me very concerned. I could fight, even make a decent showing against three; but the environment would've been my undoing. Fortunately, the leader of the little clique said something like he didn't want to soil his hands on a *piss-drinker*, and they backed off with jeers and hooting.

But when those incidents did occur, I recalled the Resurrection of the Piss Trough, and basked in the whelming pride of what I'd done. I was obsessed and my new insight, understanding of the nature of man-sex did not leave me. I held to it, claimed my nature and my kink, my obsession in all its variations. Fuck 'em, <u>none</u> I'd ever met, not even pigboy Carl in his initiation, could have approached by even a fraction the stupendous quality of my accomplishment.

And there were benefits, too. Kent had some good buddies on the track and swim teams. His chance to make Varsity was not hampered by referring a couple of leading men to me; David Southmore and David Yarrow decided they wanted to try a bit of the action. Kent and I had had an early morning work-out and were showering. I was expecting to suck him in our favorite stall when the Daves came in, Southmore in his Speedo and Yarrow in a jockstrap. They eyed us carefully, discreetly, checking out my naked body and Kent's thick dick.

Coach Thorkildsen was in his office, but he'd be busy for at least an hour; he was all but unaware of anything besides the baseball stats anyway. A group of lanky swim-jocks were simply off his radar. The men stepped into the tiled shower room with us, smiling and stroking themselves lightly. Kent grinned.

"So you made it, huh? Morning swim?"

Yarrow answered, "Well, we're thinking about water, but not in the pool, ya know?"

He eyed me suggestively, his eyes feeling me up. There was nothing wrong with his appearance either, tall and smooth, his jockstrap clean and white. The bulge was full, but the lines of balls and cock weren't distinguishable. Southmore's Speedo was a pale blue, silvery, and showed his ample meat to full advantage. He was fine, his body hair shaved, his musculature subtle but distinct. They stepped closer, and

Kent was smiling, stroking his own dick gently.

"Well, we just finished a hard work out, I'm sure we could use some refreshment. Matt's no doubt a bit thirsty after all that... huh?" He patted my back, pulling me a bit closer. They grinned in horny expectation, greedy and hot. I grinned back; wow. Kent turned to me. "Can you handle it? I told 'em you might..."

I smiled and nodded. As I grinned, I was dimly aware of a string of saliva falling from my lip. I was literally *drooling* in anticipation!

Southmore made a motion, "This way?" indicating the toilet stalls just behind the shower room. Going from the shower room itself to the pool, one would walk past a small alcove of 3 stalls, tucked in the corner. It was very discreet. I stepped toward the last one, our usual play place. They followed.

Four of us cramming into the tiny stall was a bit much, but interesting. I sat on the toilet, my legs apart to allow the new boys good access to me. They moved up close and I stroked Dave Yarrow's bulging jock. The white fabric nestled tight on him, the waistband cinching his flesh. Southmore pulled the laces on his brief and tugged the front down. His hard cock was not large, maybe 5½" but nicely shaped, a thick bush surrounding his manhood.

I slid a finger into Yarrow's pouch, and let his dick poke out. He sucked his breath in quickly, self-consciously; but made no move to pull away. Obviously he was into a bit of man-on-man fun, but probably had never done so with any but his suck-fuck buddy. Now he was in a toilet stall with 3 other guys, the intention being get his cock sucked in front of them all, and piss into another man's mouth. He was horny beyond words, but intimidated, self-conscious.

He got past it quickly enough though, and his boner sprang up nice and thick. Veins running down his shaft stood out hot and reddish: thick, impressive veins that pulsed as he began to push himself toward me. I opened my mouth and leaned to take him.

Kent was stroking Dave Southmore's dick, who wanted to join in the fun. He moved to my right, close and hot, and I managed to maneuver him so I could suck him along with his buddy. Yarrow lifted his leg, putting his left foot on my knee, stabilizing himself and holding me firmly in place. They began a slow double face fucking and I held their balls, a sac of two in each hand.

In a very few minutes, all four of us were hard and hot; Kent was the first to push forward to give me his elixir. "Um, here guys, watch this..." he said, and held his cock about 5" from my mouth. I opened wide, tilting my head back and waiting. The anticipation was wonderful, knowing that his stream at this time of the morning would be hot, salty and thick. A dribble fell from the flaring slit on his red penis, then a spurt.

Then...

Piss.

A full hot stream shot, curved up and over me, then he adjusted his aim and shot directly to the back of my throat. The Daves gasped quietly, in wonder and horny awe. I held my glottis closed and let Kent fill my mouth with his spunky yellow juice. He clenched his tube and stemmed the flow, I dramatically gulped and took the first swallow. The Daves were rapt in horny attention, Yarrow groping his hot cock and slicking it up with his own slobber to add to mine.

"Yeah man, fuckin' HOT! Oh wow, man, here..." and he aimed his dick alongside Kent's. Southmore waited, wanting to see the whole action. His dick was hard, and it took him a second to force his piss through it, overcoming the natural closing of the urethra. And when it came through, it was total. A full hard stream of thick, thick richly golden morning piss burst forth, splashing onto my face and running down my chin and onto my chest.

"FUCK man, yeah!" Southmore encouraged us, and Yarrow spurted hotter and harder. Kent opened back up and together they again filled my mouth. Kent showed the technique, gripping his penis to stop the flow and allow me to catch up. I swallowed, gulping and savoring. It was rank, thick and salty. It was all but unbelievable in its intensity, easily the heaviest piss I'd yet taken. I drank it down.

Kent stopped his flow, and pressed the small of Yarrow's back, moving him directly in front of me. "Give him your cock man, let him hold you in there, you'll love it."

Dave Yarrow straddled me, Southmore backed into the corner behind me to my right, and Kent behind Yarrow, reaching around him. I let him slide his hard penis into my lips, then he opened again, forcing his piss into me in a torrent of powerful, golden wonder. I drank, gulping as my eyes began to water.

Dave pissed and pumped into me, forcing his bladder to contract and obey; it wasn't easy, and he grunted and huffed as he fed me. But he gave it all, and I drank him down. Then Kent moved to the center, Yarrow taking the corner to my left. Southmore placed a hand on my head as Kent held away from my lips and pissed his stream from outside, showering me and feeding me as the others watched. I gulped and guzzled as I could, letting the piss flow and soak me as Kent wanted.

My own cock stood at attention, hard and dripping. My bush was soaked with their piss, and I stroked myself with their liquid gold when my hands weren't busy fondling or adjusting the men feeding me. On it went, and Kent shoved his cock into my lips, filled my mouth then arced a stream into me from afar again. It was heavenly, hot and wild. The newcomers loved it.

Kent's piss flowed, then waned to a dribble. That last shot, and he was finished. I gulped and it was Southmore's turn. Once more we adjusted position in the tiny cubicle, and Dave got over me as the others had done. He placed his hands on the sides of my head and slowly offered his cock. He was not totally hard, but thick, the size was there but I could easily move and turn him. His tube would be wide open with no difficulty.

The men touched him gently, Kent's hand on his ass, Yarrow's on his shoulder as he slid his meat to my lips. I wrapped my mouth on the tip of his cock, then sucked him in fully. I slicked him with slobber, stroking him gently, then pulled back, my lips wrapped just around the corona as I so liked. I looked up with him in my mouth. His eyes were closed.

I ran a hand up onto his body, his abdomen, and with a gentle pressure he began to feed me. I suckled, nursed slowly as he pissed as beautifully for me as if he'd been doing it for years. The stream was full, but not overwhelming. Thick and hot, his salty. Heavy piss pooled in my mouth and I slurped it down. I'd swallow, and let him fill again, and he slid his dick into my mouth a bit deeper, then pulled back to the tip again and again.

He tilted his head back, letting himself empty, fill me. He was floating in that rapt homosexual link of piss, the precious fluid of one man flowing beautifully into another, linked by cock and body, united in hot piss lust. His stream fed me, the caustic fluid burning the inside of my mouth, the vapors filling my sinus. I drank him and with a slow final dollop he too was drained. I gulped, looked up and released his hose.

"Oh fuckin' AY man, damn that was HOT!" he said. Yarrow agreed, rubbing my head. The men began to adjust, trying to see how to get the inward-swinging door open with 4 of us in there, and at last managed. Kent was kind of pushed out first, then Yarrow slipped out. Southmore was left in the stall with me, and leaned down to stroke me, grabbing my cock in his hand.

"Mmmmmm, man that was fine! Thanks!" he whispered.

"Man, thank you!" I said. "I'm into it buddy, I don't make no bones about it."

He grinned, then he too slipped out the door and went to shower off from our piss-orgy.

I would've liked to sample their sperm too, the hot semen from those guys, but leaving our contact beginning and ending in Piss was OK too. That was all we'd shared, but it spoke volumes. They were suck-fuck buddies together, and I didn't want to intrude on that turf. But they'd found something hot and new, horny and wonderful in sharing piss and that group scene with me and Kent. That was fine.

I had to let my own bladder drain and stood a moment. The heady piss I'd taken from three hot men was boiling in my guts, heavy and thick. It burned, and I burped up a thick, rancid gulp of it. I choked it back down.

Kent went to his locker, the other two got ready to get into the pool and actually have their work-out. I came out of the stall just as they were heading back through the shower room, Yarrow carrying a rolled up towel. I stopped him.

"Hey, what's that?" He looked at his gear. "That your jock? I want it man, give it to me!"

He smiled and glanced at Dave Southmore, who nodded and grinned. "OK, here." He unrolled his bundle and I took his jockstrap, adding it to my collection.

"Thanks man!" I too returned to the lockers. Kent was already dressed, and ready to leave.

"Catch you later man, swim tomorrow?"

I nodded and burped again. It was nasty.

He walked away, back out to the world and I tossed Dave Yarrow's white Champion strap into my locker. Pulling on the one I had decided to wear for the day, I had an almost uncontrollable urge and knew it would be only a few more seconds. I snapped the strap onto my body and headed back to the stall.

Kneeling in the same toilet stall we'd just had our orgy in, I leaned into the bowl and heaved. Burning, thick and powerful piss shot out, pouring in a huge splash into the water. It wasn't so much yellow as orange, almost a pale brown, hot and thick, powerful and strong. Morning piss, redolent of coffee and vitamins. I shouldn't have tried to drink it. Not that I'd have passed up the scene we'd shared, but this wasn't a smart idea. I heaved again.

Hot piss ran down my chin, and I wiped it away with my hand. One more burst and I knew I was OK. I smeared my wet hand across the front of my jockstrap, the crusty hot jock I'd taken from Bill Macey. He'd worn it at the party, and not washed it after I'd fucked him. We'd hooked up once more that week, fucking and enjoying it all. He still wasn't ready to try drinking me, but once more I'd pissed up his ass. Then I'd taken it from him, insisting it was my memento of his introduction to piss lust.

Wet and crusty now with his piss, his cum, my own fluids and Dave, Dave and Kent's piss, I wore it proudly. I wished everyone would know I had it on, but wasn't ready to wear it out on the street. Maybe someday I could manifest that kind of obsession, who knew? I dressed and went back home.

I'd drank another load from Kent 3 days later; our practice had been furious, inspired partly by the fullness of his bladder, which he held until I could drain him afterwards. We knew it was one of our last chances to have our piss-union, my graduation coming in only a few more days. He had one more year, and his swim times and the recommendations of the Daves had gotten him an auxilliary spot on the Varsity team. I'd gotten a request to stop at the Dean's office in the music building, so with Kent's piss still on my breath I headed there.

I waited a good 15 minutes before being shown in to Dean Braun's office. He sat at his massive walnut desk, pretending to be busy, keeping me on edge. It didn't work.

"Well then, Mr. Schiffmann," he began, pronouncing my name with the 'sh' sound. I corrected him, yet again. I'd had 3 classes with him, he knew better.

"It's SKIFFMAN," I said.

"Oh yes, I'm sorry. Skiffman, OK. Now then..." He took a slow breath, then began.

"We're a bit concerned here about you attending Commencement. Were you planning to attend?"

I smiled and spoke slowly. "Indeed I am, my parents are coming. You know I've worked very hard to finish my degree quickly."

"Um, yes I know. We allowed you early entrance and now you've done in 3 years. Quite commendable. However..." he paused.

"Your friendship with the Delta Tau fraternity is not so commendable. I've heard, and so have others on the faculty, some very, _very_ disturbing tales of their spring party. Do you care to tell me anything?"

Looking at him intently, I chose my words carefully, knowing this conversation might well be added to a file pertinent to admission to a graduate music academy.

"Dean Braun, I have nothing to say to you regarding events _off campus_ during a _non-academic_ week. Certain things took place, and yes, I participated with gusto. I do not know what all you may have heard, but the reality was, I am absolutely sure, far less disturbing that you think."

He wasn't convinced, not by a long shot.

"I keep certain friends in all the fraternity houses. Maybe you're not aware of that fact, but I do. And I have what I am certain is accurate, convincing information regarding the events at that party. Right down to the false wall and a urinal stolen from the University Stadium. I am shocked, utterly shocked by all of it. And we are going to be disbanding the Delta house because of this. But that is not your concern."

He leaned back, his paunch intended to awe and cow me. His pale blue eyes searched me for some sign of penitence, of being shamed or embarrassed. After the glorious epiphany of that trough, which I now recalled in glowing clarity, he was not going to steal the glory of it from me. Fuck that.

"What is of concern is that we do not want some kind of a homo-rights scene at the Commencement. There are bound to be many others who are aware of what happened that night. And both pro- and con-, they are going to be there to carry on when your name is called and you walk across the platform. I won't have it. You are _not_ to attend graduation."

I looked at him intently, once more choosing words very carefully. He added one more thought.

"Tell your family and friends you're sick. Get yourself good and 'sick' on Friday night, and stay home. Go drink a bellyful of piss and stay in bed on Saturday, got it?" he said, dripping contempt. I stared back at him with equal disgust.

"No. I most certainly will _not_ do that." I began. His mouth fell open in shock; _nobody_ ever contradicted him! It was bizarre.

"I am going to walk across there with the rest of my class and collect my diploma, sir. Our division has over 600 students graduating, and I'm not going to give up my 8 seconds on the stage either. You'll hand me my certificate, and I'll go off into the hills and that will be that. But I am attending."

He glared, and tried once more.

"That is not going to happen. If you show up, we will prevent you from joining the line. We are not going to have the _scene_ and the jeering, the catcalls and the _shame_ that you will bring upon us..." I stopped him.

"Yes you will; and if you stop me, there will be serious consequences. I will go directly from that line to my lawyer's office. And by Monday, I will have filed some weighty papers. I will sue. I will sue the University, the Music School, the State of Minnesota and I will sue YOU personally. The Student Handbook states that off-campus activities cannot be cited as a basis for discipline, especially when school is not in session. If you really think it's worth all that, go ahead. I'm not denying anything, I'm not admitting anything, but I AM going to be in that line on Saturday morning."

I rose from the chair and once more the Dean sat dumbfounded.

"Good day Dean Braun, and thank you for your leadership and instruction these past 3 years." I turned and walked out of his office. As I gathered my jacket and things in the outer office, once more I burped slightly, The flavor and scent of Kent's piss filled my mouth and nostrils. I thought to myself, regarding the Dean and his comments:

"If you only knew asshole, if you only knew about it." I left, my yellow jockstrap wrapped snugly about me beneath my clothes.

I wore it to Commencement, too. In fact, since Mace gave it to me I wore it almost constantly, my own secret symbol of my transformation. But as my jockstrap collection grew, I couldn't help but wear them... there were some favorites, but they all had to get their turns in action.

Graduation went without a hitch. I dressed in my gown and mortarboard and strolled into the auditorium with the rest of the graduates. I passed the line of faculty, the Marshal and provost, Dean Braun and the whole crew. Nobody said a thing. We were seated, listened to the droll speeches and comments, the roster was called. My turn came and my line proceeded to the stage; and I walked up. I handed a slip of paper with my name to the receiver as Donna Schaefer was given her Bachelor of Music degree, her claque responding with loud cheering and congratulations, then it was my turn.

I approached and the Dean glared as my name was read into the microphone. A chorus of cheers went up, Kent and many others. Sex buddies, tutors, those I'd coached. My family and friends. I heard only the cheering as I accepted my diploma; I was told later there were calls of "pig!" and "faggot," but we were unaware of them. It was done.

We went to an early dinner, my family and a few friends. Kenton did not attend, I think he in fact was too embarrassed, but it wasn't an issue. I was toasted and feted, the new graduate. My older brother wasn't too pleased. At 19, he was just finishing his first year of university up in Grand Forks, North Dakota. His semester ended in another 3 weeks. But a chapter in life was over; and I had to get on with things. I had a summer job lined up, a silly 'assistant manager' thing at the truck stop. I would decide about graduate school during the summer. For now, life was good.

Finishing my dinner, I went to the restroom and paused a moment. The urinal on the wall was exactly the shape of those at the stadium, from the same manufacturer. I was loving the irony as I got into position, then another man entered the room and took the place beside me. I could just see as he pulled his dick out and slowly began to piss. It was yellow, redolent of pheromones and masculinity as it poured from his fine cock. He didn't pay any attention to me, and I watched him drain with fondness and fascination.

Piss.

I tucked myself back into my jockstrap and returned to our table.

My Obsessions went on.

UNEXPECTED COMPANY

Life settled into its routine after graduation. I had very little time to be idle, as my job would start the week following. But I did have a few days to myself. I enjoyed them, taking stock and preparing for the summer. Kent went back to his home; I remained in Minneapolis. Perhaps I'd see him in the fall, maybe even in the summer. We made no plans or promises, but parted friends.

I packed up much of my student gear and library; I did not intend to work on academia or even music during the summer. I spent all Friday loading books and memorabilia into boxes, stacking it along the wall of the living room. I cleaned and rearranged the place. I was tired, and went to bed early, falling into a deep satisfied sleep.

The doorbell startled me awake, and a glance to the clock told me it was only 6:03 AM. What the hell? Who? I grabbed a robe as I stumbled to the door. The light of dawn was nice, shadowy and sensuous. Peering out the peephole I didn't recognize the man at the door. I opened it slowly. "Yeah?"

He stood nervously, hesitant. He was obviously a bit loaded, possibly still going from the night before. Wow. He smiled, then spoke. "I'm Joe. You know... Kent's buddy? We've met..."

"Oh yeah, OK. I remember." I didn't remember at all, and I wondered why not. He was very nice looking; a bit on the lanky side, but quite nice. About 5'6 and maybe 140 pounds, dark hair and a well-trimmed goatee. He shifted his weight to the other side. "What's up?"

He chuckled nervously. "Well, I just wondered what you're up to... kinda looking for a little company for a minute you know...?"

I smiled. Kent sent him; oh well. A trick showing up at the door unannounced on a Saturday morning wasn't all bad. At least I was sober. I nodded, then opened the door fully. "C'mon in."

He brushed against me lightly as he entered, then quickly took off his jacket. Again he shifted from one foot to the other. He stroked the bulge in his jeans. Nicely defined, I could see the outline of a decent sized dick in there. He wanted attention.

"You need some help with that?" I asked. I stroked the front of his jeans, gripping his cock in my hand.

"Ugggh," he groaned. "Oh..." He winced.

"What's the matter? I didn't hurt you did I?"

"Um, no man... it's not that. It's just... well..." he paused a moment. I held that bulge very lightly and his cock pulsed behind the denim.

"I really gotta piss man, I'm full."

"Yeah?" I asked, a bit stunned. "You don't say..."

"Yeah I do man, big time. I can barely hold it any longer. Kent told me... he said you... um... he said you like to get into that..."

"Well yeah Joe, I do. This is kind of a surprise though..."

"Yeah I guess so. He told me where you live. But man... I gotta GO. You wanna do it or not?"

"Sure thing Joe, I want to take it. You ever done this before?"

"No man, Kent said it's really hot though. Where? WHERE?" He was unzipping.

Quickly I stepped toward the bathroom and flopped my robe aside. My cock was already ¾ hard and I was ready. This was *Hot!* A damn stranger showing up at the door to feed me... God love ya, Kent! He followed me into the bathroom. I stepped into the tub and knelt.

"You got any poppers?" I motioned to the top of the toilet, and instantly he grabbed the bottle and twisted the cap; already a dribble was beginning to flow from his cockhead. I leaned forward and took hold of his dick. He wasn't large, about 4" soft, but nice, veiny and thick. His bush was redolent of manscent as I wrapped my lips around his corona. He huffed, and without another sound his piss gushed forth.

And damn did it gush... I gulped, struggled to take it and gulped again. I choked and passed a wad of piss out my nostrils. I had to drop his cock and hack a bit. The hot flow hosed onto my chest and he moaned.

"Oh man, don't stop! Drink it man, please... *Please*! Drink me!" Quickly I recovered and leaned forward. I held his cock and tightened my grip, controlling the flow. He moaned again and swiveled his hips gently. The flow was stanched a bit and I began to enjoy the action, savoring. His piss was thick, hot, thick and delicious. This wasn't beer piss after a long night of drinking: the guy had gone home, slept a bit, *then* got up and had a beer and decided Kent's suggestion was something he needed to try. I drank, my eyes half closed.

I tightened my grip as I nestled his taut ballsac in my left hand. I held his cock out, the flow stopped and I motioned for the bottle. "Let's hit it again."

He held the open bottle, his thumb blocking the top. He lifted it and huffed, then held it toward me. I took a hit in either nostril, then opened my mouth. Taking the head of his now-growing dick into my mouth, I relaxed the grip on his tube. The flow resumed, full force, and I gulped insanely, loving it. I drank and nursed, savored and swallowed.

"Oh yeah man, yeah! Take it! Oh man! Yeah buddy... yeah... Take my *piss!*" He moaned and pissed. And pissed and pissed... and kept pissing.

The rush swam through my head and I controlled his flow, savoring the beauty of it. I still couldn't believe it: this nice stranger coming to the door, full and ready. I didn't have to hint or beat around the bush, try to get past his weird inhibitions, get him drunk or stoned and beg for it. He was ready: he wanted new perversions, the new rush, new action. I drank more, alternately tightening and loosening my grip, making him piss slowly. He liked it too, letting me control his achingly-full bladder as I drained him.

It was heavenly, and kneeling in the shadowy bathroom once more I remembered that first night when Dean forced me to take his piss. His piss... his hot, holy Piss. Oh god, *piss*. Dean... Johann... Mace... Now Joe. Oh god. Piss for me man, give it to me. Oh thank you, Joe! Thank you, Kent! Piss for me buddy...

I savored it and guzzled, letting his cock hang loose and wide open in my mouth. Now that the initial force was abated, I could take it straight on and just let him drain. He was standing in front of me, rushing in the poppers and wallowing in the sensations. Pouring his manly juice into another man, feeding me as only a man can. He instinctively understood the deep connection, his fluid filling me, his essence being transferred from his body into mine.

The flow slackened, then stopped. One more nice pulse, one last spurt, and he was done.

"Oh man, fuckin' ay... Wow," he stammered. "WOW! That was hot." He pulled back and tugged his cock and began to straighten himself up.

"Yeah man, HOT! Thanks Joe. C'mon, let me enjoy some more of that dick..."

"Um, well Matt... I really don't got time. I'm not..." He paused.

"What?" I asked, puzzled.

"I'm not into guys. I'm married. I just... I... well, I just needed to try..." He trailed off.

I was really shocked now. A _straight_ guy, married! One of Kent's buddies somehow, but he was a close enough pal to know about cock-sucking, butt-fucking and _Piss!_ Wow! I was floored.

"No shit!" I smiled, then laughed gently. "OK man, I don't mind. That was really hot..." I got up from the bottom of the tub and stood.

He smiled and exhaled heavily. "Goddam buddy, Kent said you were cool. I was afraid you'd be mad that I don't wanna do anything else." He exhaled again, then almost whispered, "Thanks Matt..."

He was genuinely relieved. I smiled again, then stroked the front of his Levi's gently.

"Hey man, it's OK, I _enjoyed_ it. Did you? Did you like it? Was it what you'd thought it would be?"

He put an arm around me and pulled me in for a quick hug. He didn't let my naked body rub him <u>too</u> closely, but patted my ass, then broke away. "OH MAN, it was great! I didn't know it could be that hot, but I'd thought about it. I wanted Cathy to try it, but she... she... she was grossed out."

"Um, I don't know about that, but I'd think another guy would be better anyhow..."

"Yeah, Kent said that too. I think you're right. That was HOT. I'm just not into, you know, the rest... what you guys are into." I nodded.

I licked my lips and said, "Yeah that's cool. I understand. I know you're a straight man; it's ok. But there's a bit of connection only guys can share."

"Yeah!" he smiled. "That's it. It's a guy thing!" We both laughed.

"It sure is!"

"Anyhow Matt, thanks. I really, _really_ got off with that. I just... I knew it would be great. I just wondered if..."

I stopped him. "I know man! It's fine! Really! If you want, we _can_ do more."

"God yeah! I was hoping we could. I come by this way maybe on Tuesdays and Sunday mornings, right about 6:00. I work over at Bancroft's." He meant a small plastics plant not 2 miles from the apartment. So he was on a night shift, and we could have us a nice little affair. A hot little arrangement beginning and ending in piss. His cock, his piss; my mouth and willing soul. Damn right!

"Fuck yeah Joe! That'll be great. Anytime you like buddy, anytime. I can give you my number." He nodded and grinned. "But I was wondering man, when did we meet? Did Kent introduce us or what? I'm sorry but I really _don't_ remember..."

It was Joe's turn to chuckle. "Um Matt... we didn't. I lied. Kent's been telling me about this buddy of his, who gets into piss. The more I heard, the more I wanted to know. I begged him to tell me who you were. Finally a couple weeks ago we were at the Legion. He got half loaded and I managed to get your address and phone number from him."

I laughed out loud. "And you had the BALLS to come over here and expect me to drink you dry first thing in the morning?!?! Damn buddy! I like you!"

"Well, I had to really get stewed up to come by. I went home, tried to ignore it but I couldn't sleep. More I thought about it, more I wanted it. Finally I had to. Just had to."

"Well then if you already got my number..."

"Yeah I do. And I'll call. But what I was wondering though is, I got an idea... something else I'd really like to try."

"What's that?"

"Well, I'm on a weird shift. I get off work tonight around 2:00. I'd like to come over..."

"OK, yeah...?"

"And maybe just come in. You know, the door unlocked?"

I nodded, my mind reeling. For a straight boy, he sure had a hot homo fantasy worked up! I loved it.

"You bet man... maybe just find me in the dark? Or a real dim light, like a candle or something?"

"Yeah, something like that. I just wanna come in, go into the bathroom like we did, but totally dark. I'll unzip and stick my dick out, and you suck it. Suck my dick and drink my piss and that's all. I'll zip up and leave. I really would like that man, it'll turn me ON!"

"You got it Joe, I'll be ready. Door unlocked, place dark, me thirsty...

you got it."

"Man! Man..." He sighed again. "I'll be here at 2:05, and full. I can hold more than I had now." That was saying a lot, and I noticed the full hard-on he was now sporting in those jeans.

"Fuck yeah man, bring it on! I'll be ready!" I wanted to ask one more thing. "Um, Joe?" He looked at me, quizzically.

"Wear a jockstrap, OK?" He grinned.

"Yeah, OK man, you got it!" Again it was instinctive. He'd gladly indulge my other obsession to satisfy his now-acknowledged craving for piss-play. He hugged me quickly once more, then walked to the door. He picked up his jacket and gave one last wink as he left. "TONIGHT MAN! *TONIGHT*!" I couldn't wait.

The only light on was the small nightlight in the entry. Coming into the apartment, you could just see the hallway, and going around the corner the bathroom door was in total darkness. I had everything ready and the door unlocked. I'd put on my spunky yellow jockstrap and was waiting, my heart racing as I anticipated the hot scene to come. I glanced around the apartment one last time, and the glow of the digital clock showed 2:03... no, 2:04. I peeked out the window and noticed a small dark sedan pulling into the parking lot. I tugged the door and it was just ajar in the frame, ready.

Quickly I went into the bathroom and got into the tub, on my knees. I held a brand-new bottle of poppers in my hand, my cock thick and hard in my strap. There was a slight noise, then a click. The door opened, then closed. Another click told me it was locked. A few very muffled footsteps and then a shadow in the dark doorway, the outline of a shortish man. His arms obviously moved to the front of his pants. He stepped into the room.

I coughed very lightly as he approached, then took a heavy hit from the bottle. I reached up and my hand touched the front of his jock, brushing against his. I nudged him with the bottle and he took it as my hand found his cock. He was almost totally hard. I guided him towards me, opening my mouth and touching my tongue to the slit of his dickhead as he huffed the poppers. He stepped up to the edge of the tub, as close as he could. I took the head of his cock into my mouth and cupped his balls in my hand as I'd done that morning. I waited for the first rush, and it was not long in coming.

With a light moan, Joe let himself wooze in the rush and relax. There was a drop, then a slow spurt, then...

The rush. Oh god.

Piss.

Piss. It gushed out and I gulped, intending to let him simply piss as hot and hard as he liked. I held my hands against the flat belly, stroking his body hair as my other hand caressed his balls. I gulped and guzzled, drank it down. He moaned again and gently pushed himself forward, pissing. Pissing. Oh man, it ran, it flowed, I couldn't take it all. The hot piss gushed around my mouth and ran down my chin, soaking my scruffy beard.

I let it run down my chest and onto my jock. My cock jumped and throbbed. I had to slow him down, and gripped the shaft of his dick behind his strap. He moaned again, liking that even better. It would make it last longer for us both.

I drank, gulping mouthfuls of Joe's piss. I'd let my mouth fill till I could barely hold another drop, then gulped and let him fill me again. On and on it went, he wasn't kidding when he'd said he could hold more. He pissed. Oh fuck he PISSED. And I drank. Mmmmmmmmm... yes I did.

I reached up and took the poppers from his hand, and he quickly gripped the base of his dick, stopping his flow. He waited while I took a hit, then retrieved the bottle and took one himself, then we repositioned and continued. He began to piss again, and once more I sucked and savored his output. I relaxed in the rush and opened my own valve, and began to piss in my jockstrap while I knelt and suckled from Joe's fine cock.

Some babies are breast-fed. Others are bottle babies. I nursed and sucked; a cock baby.

A piss baby. The more I drank from Joe, the more I liked it. The hotter and prouder I became. I loved it. I drank.

He pissed for a solid 2 minutes, more. On and on, and I took it. The small amount that ran down my chest and chin was just enough to wet me, and the load I pissed on myself completed the job. I was soaked and sated. I sucked again, taking Joe's last drops. He moaned, then began to slide himself into my mouth, in and out. A nice slow rhythm, and I kept sucking as his cock strained and pulsed, now totally hard. He began to ooze and I tasted a hint of precum.

I didn't dare say anything, as he's said do this in the darkness, just piss and zip up, go. But he didn't pull back, so I sucked. He began to thrust a bit harder and then, the low growl of impending orgasm. I sucked and slurped, letting him set the pace and fuck my face. He thrust in hard, as deep as his cock could go. Hard he was maybe 5 ½ or 6 inches; nice and proportionate. Hot and oozing and hard enough to cut diamonds. I could easily take him to the balls, let him drill in and hold while he shot his wad. He bucked, then he came.

Spurt, gulp. Spurt, gulp... I let him pump his jizz into my mouth and received it gladly. He thrust again, gave me that last delicious morsel, then pulled back. With a low sigh he yanked his cock up, back into his jock, zipped up his jeans and spun toward the door. I saw the silhouette once more as he turned and headed back down the hall. Tromp, tromp, tromp, click... slam. And he was gone without a word.

I knelt in the tub a long, long moment, savoring the piss-cum in my mouth. The puddle of my own piss on the floor of the tub, the wetness of my jockstrap. I closed my eyes and swooned; god. Oh GOD! *Yes! YES!* He'd be back. Now I knew it for sure. He'd even accepted my blowjob, gave me his sperm. He wanted more, obviously.

After a minute or two, I began to get a bit chilly. Time to recover, go jack off and remember it all. I went to the couch in the living room, leaving only that nightlight glowing. I pulled my fat cock from my jockstrap and began to stroke. A gob of spit in my hand slicked things up and I was within a few seconds of blowing my own load when the phone rang. Of course it was Joe.

"Hello?"

"Matt? Goddam man... *GODDAM!* Thank you! Man you fuckin' cocksucker, thank you!"

"Oh fuck man, thank *you*! That was fucking HOT. Anytime buddy, any time you want."

"Man I know... you've showed me something fantastic! Goddam I loved that! I can't wait to do more! Man, I can't fucking wait! But I can't work it out till Tuesday. I get off at 6... I'll be by 5 minutes later, OK? Tuesday? Tuesday morning?"

"Sure man, sure thing! I'll be ready. Same deal? Lights out, no words?"

"Um... I dunno. Not sure man..."

"OK Joe, I know what you want. I'll be ready, just like tonight. You come in, give me your cock and you take the lead. Give me your piss, give me your cum if you want. You wanna talk, you talk. I won't say nothing till you do ok? We'll just let it happen..."

"PERFECT, man! Perfect! I'll see you then."

I could barely wait myself, and stroked my dick slowly as I recalled the hot, pouring piss from Joe's rock-hard tool. My cock was silhouetted by the small nightlight as I stretched back on the couch; I tugged my strap to the side and let my balls hang free as I jacked. Spitting a gob into my hand I slicked myself as the droplets sparkled on my wet chest hair, wet with Joe's piss. I groaned softly as my slit flared and my cock throbbed.

A gleaming droplet of precum oozed out, and I twisted my hand across my cockhead to mix it onto my lube. I gripped my cock at the base, forcing my full 8" to stand upright, a powerful dark shadow in the seductive light. I admired and compared myself to other, beautiful cocks I'd known: I wasn't as large as Dean, but this was fine in any case. I worked myself and neared cumming, holding my balls as I pumped up and down.

My bush was wet with Joe's fine output, and I ground my hand onto his piss and my own sweat too. The sensations of rubbing my swollen, red corona and the stroking of my shaft, with the scent and taste of Joe's piss finally pushed me to the edge. I groaned, growled and bucked my hips upward as my cock shot a thick arc of cum up onto my chest.

I gasped softly in the dim light, and two, three more bursts of sperm spurted up, a thick strand running down the back of my hand as I finished masturbating. Mmmmmm, *piss,* Joe's piss; cocks and cum, piss and jockstraps. Once more I recalled the clarity of my Epiphany in the piss trough, and I realized anew the beauty of my obsessions. There would be more; oh indeed there would be. The convulsions in my prostate subsided and I sank onto the sofa in satisfaction.

I simply sailed in the joy of my orgasm for long moments, my legs stretched forward as I reclined. Coated with piss, sticky with cum, my cock slowly softened. I could see the white numbers on the clock flip to 2:39 when I finally hauled myself up and headed to bed.

Without even bothering about 'cleaning up,' I slid into bed crusty and scented. I daubed a small gob of my own semen from my chest and licked it from my fingertip, and almost instantly fell fast asleep. My hand was stuck to the pillowcase with dried cum when I awoke the following morning. My yellow jockstrap was fused to my body as I stretched awake, ready for the beginning of summer, ready for more piss.

AUTHOR'S NOTE

I am quite sure it will be obvious to most readers that the events, characters and locations depicted in _The Yellow Jock Chronicles_ are for the most part genuine. And as usual, names have been changed, dates and locations modified. Some are composites, others purely fictional creations suggested by one or more real person, place or event. That's the beauty of retelling what is, in greatest part, a true story, but with the license to adapt and modify according to literary need.

Resemblance to real persons, living or dead, is a matter of degree. Those persons most responsible for and most involved in the actual events described herein may or may not recognize themselves and others. But to them and to all, I wish to say that no offense is intended in descriptions of human weakness, mistakes or deeds which may have caused anyone harm or distress. The events are far in the past; those who would fault me for the fictionalized version of what might or might not have happened in real time need to find something else to bitch about.

I ask readers to take the book for what it is: the reflections of one person put into a kind of context that may or may not make sense to others. In the meanwhile, I hope what I have set out is an entertaining and enjoyable story, if not one which a particular reader can relate to or derive any new "enlightenment" or such therefrom.

Those who read this account with an open mind and interest in their own predilections will, I think, relate to the struggles and the dawning self-awareness I have tried to describe. Perhaps my *Chronicles* will give cause for reflection, perhaps it's just a good wild pornographic story... but I ask readers to realize that while what I have written may have been "real," it is presented through an admittedly very selective filtering process.

Some events are presented quite accurately, others as they "should have" happened, still others as I "wish" they had happened; and lastly, some events and characters are nothing but the fruit of a beautifully perverse and creative imagination, "fiction" in the purest sense.

M. M. Schiffmann

Richmond, Virginia

ABOUT THE AUTHOR

Matthew Schiffmann has been publishing books and articles since the mid-1970's under several names. An accomplished professional musician, Dr. Schiff has performed across the US and Canada as both pianist and conductor. His published writings range from social and political science materials to theological analyses, poetry and fiction. His homo-erotic fiction resumes after a long hiatus with the release of _The Yellow Jock Chronicles_.

From very small-town roots through advanced studies in major Universities and academies, Schiff has an extremely wide background. The range of his interests can be surprising: he has earned citations in automobile and motorcycle restorations, professional tailoring, business projects involving major automobile manufacturers and international banking, and is accomplished in several other fields. His students have generally regarded him as one of the most formative figures in their education. He has taught subjects ranging from mathematics and natural sciences, music, to classical languages and theology, spanning classrooms from kindergarten through doctoral–level students.

Dr. Schiffmann's social involvement includes working for removing barriers based upon sexual orientation, and has served in top-level consultation for State and local government agencies. He is currently working with the Equality Project, and is producing the framework and legal basis for major civil-rights litigation.

Matthew Schiffmann is also the author of:

> *The Yellow Jock Chronicles - Volume Two: Jockstrap Branded A Journey into Self-Awareness, Discovery and Acceptance: Further Obsession with Jockstraps and Piss-Lust*

> (978-1-934625-30-9, The Nazca Plains Corp., 2007)

Available from Amazon.com, Goodboner.com, or your local bookstore.

www.ingramcontent.com/pod-product-compliance
Lightning Source LLC
Chambersburg PA
CBHW071212260626
47162CB00004B/1266